BY THE GRACE OF GOD

BY THE GRACE OF GOD

A NOVEL

KESHIA DAWN

www.urbanchristianonline.net

URBAN BOOKS
1199 Straight Path
West Babylon, NY 11704

ISBN- 13: 978-1-60162-962-3
ISBN- 10: 1-60162-962-1

First Printing July 2008
Printed in the United States of America

10 9 8 7 6 5 4 3 2 1

This is a work of fiction. Any references or similarities to actual events, real people, living, or dead, or to real locales are intended to give the novel a sense of reality. Any similarity in other names, characters, places, and incidents is entirely coincidental.

Distributed by Kensington Publishing Corp.
Submit Wholesale Orders to:
Kensington Publishing Corp.
C/O Penguin Group (USA) Inc.
Attention: Order Processing
405 Murray Hill Parkway
East Rutherford, NJ 07073-2316
Phone: 1-800-526-0275
Fax: 1-800-227-9604

Acknowledgments:

GOD is good, may be cliché to some, but to me it's a statement of all statements. I'm blessed to even write this page of acknowledgments. Amazement is still running warm in my veins as I pinch myself and realize I've done what my heart desired.

I give honor to my God in heaven for gracing me with the gift to tell the stories He's given my heart. It's not as easy as it seems to put words in a sentence and a sentence in a paragraph and paragraphs into a page. But all things are possible with God our Father. Thank you, my Lord and Savior, for never leaving me throughout my life's experience and pointing me to my destiny. You are my Father. I thank you, Lord!

Family is important, so much that I'd like to acknowledge the family of which I'm a part. My parents and my younger sisters Fanasha and Angel. Fanasha, thank you for taking the role of big sister during my pregnancy and putting up with my whining when I was *so* through with being pregnant—LOL! Love you . . . my first baby! Thanks go to my daughter, Chayse Karyngton-Dawn, Mommy loves you with her whole being. You are the best baby ever. Thank you for being my inspiration to pick up the pen once more.

To my extended family, my cousins in particular, those I see often and those I don't, I love you and thank you for the support over the years. You've always been my cheerleaders and I cherish you for that! Kim, you are strong and people will only understand you when they themselves become real. I love the realness with you!

To the Pratt and Sauls family, thank you for being the blood that runs warm through my veins. Somehow you've made me into the writer that I am and I am grateful for you all.

To the Crenshaw (Ms. Crenshaw) and Hunt family (Aunt Bobbie and Uncle T), thank you for allowing me to be a part of your lives for all these years, attached and detached. I honestly love you for the welcome! Ms. Crenshaw, you'll always be loved by myself and Chayse. The way you think of us often is a blessing!

Some people think that I love my friends a little too much. I call it a blessing to have friends that have become family to me. To have communication and a loving, emotional relationship is awesome! Alex and Shakira, thank you for being an inspiration and praising my work and accepting the role of godparents toward my Chayse-ee. Rodney, Yolanda, and the boys, thank you for throwing my very first, *By the Grace of God* surprise party when I self-published. You all are the example of what God meant for husband and wife. Even though I don't see you often, you are always on my mind.

The legacy of my family runs more than three generations in the COGIC church. I want to thank Bishop J. Neul and First Lady Vivian Haynes along with the Saintsville Sanctuary Church of God In Christ in Dallas.

Thank you for promoting me when I first self-published. I'm grateful! As well, I'm blessed that God has moved me to Greater Zion Temple in Temple, Texas where I'm under the tutelage of Superintendent Shelton C. Rhodes and his wife Missionary Deborah A. Rhodes. The teachings from both of you have molded me and helped move me to my next level. Thank you.

I must, must, must give a shout out to those who have accepted me in the world of writing. Starting in 2003 when I self-published, I had the opportunity to be amongst some great writers and in some great writing groups. Wanda D. Hudson, I have to thank you for helping me make sense out of all the mumbo jumbo that sat on my computer. You were my editor before I knew what an editor was. My freelance editor, Shonell Bacon, who did a wonderful job making me really feel like an author. Thank you! Toschia, for being the first "author friend," and giving me the low-down on how to work book signings! Sister Friend Writers, Black Christian Writers, Fiction Folk Writers . . . big ups to you and all the help that you've given relentlessly throughout the years.

Most recently, when I was determined to pick up the pen again, I found THE HUT. Writers Hut, an on-line writing group, headed by *Essence* best-selling author, Kendra Norman-Bellamy, is the best I've come across. Not to mention the most open and honest group of individuals that I've come across in a looooong time! Big ups to you!

Elissa Gabrielle, thank you for sharing my story in *The Triumph of My Soul,* thanks for loving my story!

And thanks for allowing inspiration to pour through Peace In the Storm Publishing.

Most definitely I'd like to thank my publisher: Urban Christian, Carl Weber, and editor, Joylynn Jossel! Thank you for picking up the telephone and welcoming me into the family! The best is yet to come for Urban Christian!

There is a group of ladies that will become closer to me than most starting July 2008! *Literarily Saved* is a Christian tour group that developed, and thanks to God, these women have brought their expertise, their fiction and non-fiction Christian literature and molded . . . our tour. Fon James, Mikasenoja, Cheryl Donovan, and Betty Knight-Allen. Check us out at www.literarily-savedontour.com

If I missed you, it was not on purpose and know that I acknowledge you in my heart, which is more than any paper can do! Please stay tuned, because it's not over until God says it's over!

Love,
Keshia Dawn

Dedications:

Superintendent F.T. Pratt Sr. (deceased)
Missionary Ella Dean Pratt (deceased)
Earl Lee Sauls (deceased)
Georgia Sauls: 85 years young

Special Dedication:

This book is dedicated to my Aunt Lillian Brooks
(Tee-Lee). For I think of you daily and with that I'm
thankful to have known you and the knowledge that
you held. Instead of gossip, you'd give a Bible
scripture. I'm proud to have been often mistaken for
your daughter. You made a spot for Chayse, and I'm
ever grateful. Your spirit will forever be felt within!
The Pratt family will always need you. Paris is
missing you! God has you! Loving you!

PROLOGUE

"**D**illian, I just know you are not about to go sleep on the couch again! What is wrong with you?" Leaning against the threshold of the master bathroom's entrance, Gracie stood with her hands in her hair as her fiancé gathered a pillow, and a blanket and headed for the bedroom door.

"Oh no. I'm going to surf the net for a bit and watch some television. I don't want to disturb you, Gracie. Go ahead and get some rest, babe," Dillian answered.

"Dillian!" Gracie looked down at her practically new ivory satin nightgown; she let him know she didn't want rest. "Does it look as if I'm trying to be alone in bed tonight, again? What is really going on?" Gracie gave her head a slight tilt.

"Honey, I've told you that I can't be doing all of that." Realizing that the look on her face wouldn't be replaced with solace so easily, Dillian walked toward Gracie. "Look, my knee is still acting up and I don't want to take any chances at making matters worse. I still have to go to the doctor's office." Placing a kiss on her right temple, Dillian waited to see if his effort would pay off.

"But that's just it. You've already gone. You told me you're okay."

Dillian switched the body-sized pillow to the opposite armpit, scratched the top of his head, and started in.

"Yeah, I said I was okay, but not fine. I'm going to get a second opinion. Look Gracie, I really am getting tired now. I'll be to bed later . . . go on and get some sleep."

With that excuse lingering in the air, Gracie left the room but questioned herself.

Just how many opinions are you trying to get for one knee?

Without hesitation, Gracie watched Dillian returned to her cozy restroom and slowly changed into her favorite pair of five-year-old cotton pajamas; figuring if she had to sleep in her king-sized bed alone, she might as well get comfortable. Gracie knelt to say a quick prayer before climbing into her bed, staring off into the night before finding her sleep.

CHAPTER ONE

Gracie started her day as normal as the next. With the stretches and pulls she forced on her limbs, she led her determined pupils in their warm-up routine at six o'clock in the morning.

"One, two, three, four. Again, one, two . . ." Gracie Gregory loved what she did even if she started her day before six o'clock in the morning. All of the success in her dream job didn't come by hard work, but by a mere accident.

If it hadn't been for the pulled and destroyed muscle in her leg that had her admitted into the hospital instead of signed up for the Summer Olympics, Gracie would have never found her career as an aerobics instructor. At the young age of twenty-two, Gracie's hard efforts suddenly put an end to her life-long dream: she stretched too hard on an already-worn tendon. The ultimate competition that Gracie had forever dreamed of was no longer an option.

That disappointment was four years ago, and soon after, instead of sulking through her "should've, could've, would've" syndrome, a determined Gracie put pen to paper while still in the hospital and went to plan 'B': her own business.

With a grand idea in mind and money lent from her supportive parents and godparents, Gracie opened her very own fitness workout center two years later and named it Full of Grace Fitness Gym, a place both men and women could frequent. Be it running, swimming, or even wall climbing, Gracie's gym had it all and gave its consumers their money's worth, right in the heart of Dallas.

Since she didn't have the sources to fully staff and run the unique and fulfilling gym alone, Gracie decided to accept freelancing instructors and took on a business partner. Gracie could think of no one better qualified to become partner of her gym than her loyal best friend, Kendra.

For one, both had been health nuts since their track days at the university in Texas, blending perfectly together. But it was more than just their shared interest. It was instinct.

For Gracie, it was more on the level of being able to totally trust Kendra. Since Kendra was a friend through sunny days and gray skies, the support she showed as confidant, more like a sister, had always stayed with Gracie.

Just like when Gracie's turmoil grew in her committed relationship with Dillian, 'crazy Kendra' as Gracie called her, was there to help her through, no matter what.

Walking into the shared office, Gracie greeted a seated Kendra. "Hey, girl."

"What's going on, Gracie? I thought you said you were going to change your hours after the summer?" Kendra responded to a half-energized Gracie.

"Yeah, I thought so too. But since things aren't getting any better on the home front, the more I stay away, it seems to be best." Gracie took a drink of her bottled water before sinking into the vacant sofa.

"You mean to tell me he's still acting strange? What's up with him, yo?"

Gracie smiled and shook her head at Kendra. Even though they were both born and raised in Texas and had Texas accents, Kendra loved to use her bits and pieces of East Coast slang that she picked up from her East Coast boyfriend, Sean.

"Honestly, I don't know. He paged me and said he wanted to get together during my first break and talk." With their relationship already on the brink of death, Gracie knew things between her and Dillian were just about over. "I'm wondering if I should even go."

Kendra, noticing distress in Gracie's brown eyes, felt that Gracie needed a hug. She rose from her recliner and offered her friend a supportive embrace. Kendra knew even if it was the end of their relationship, Gracie and Dillian needed to talk.

From the beginning, Kendra had seen the love that Dillian had for Gracie and vice versa. She had been thrown for a loop as well when issues developed in their relationship and threw them off course. Yet and still, Kendra knew that she had to be the shoulder when Gracie needed to cry.

"You can't just *not* talk to him, Gracie. Whatever it is, good or bad, you need to know. If he is not the man that is supposed to be your husband, you need to know so that you don't waste any more time on the relationship." Kendra tried to keep her eyes on Gracie as she picked up her workout towel and CDs.

"I know," was all that Gracie could muster up.

Kendra stood beside the door, watching the array of emotions gather on Gracie's face. "Are you going to be okay, girl?" Kendra asked. "I have a class in about two minutes, but . . ."

"Yeah," Gracie lied, as she offered Kendra a weak smile. "Go on. I'll talk to you later, but thanks for listening."

Kendra gave Gracie a parting smile before leaving. As the door shut, Gracie slid off the sofa and reached for her two-way on the table.

For the next fifteen minutes, Gracie and her beau fought to set up the time they needed to put aside to have their "talk."

"Is this not something that can wait until I make it home from work?" Gracie paged Dillian.

"No! So are you coming or not?" Dillian responded.

When they couldn't agree on a time that suited both of their schedules, they both responded with *"fine."*

Gracie knew she couldn't neglect her eight o'clock class with her paying customers just because Dillian didn't have any clients at that time slot. Her routine was just as important as his.

Six o'clock was her first class: fifty minutes with a fifteen-minute cool down. Next, she had a forty-five minute break that Dillian wanted her to rush home during. That time was consciously set aside for greetings and questions. After that, her next class started promptly at eight o'clock. She had a schedule, and she wasn't breaking it.

Assuming that he would be at the apartment, Gracie made up her mind to go home for lunch to see if he really wanted to talk. If so, she knew he'd be there at twelve.

Gracie rubbed her face and let out a long, wistful sigh. "How did things get like this?" she asked the empty office. Her mind whirled as she tried to come up with an answer. She couldn't figure it out. It had only been six months since she and Dillian had made one of the biggest steps a couple could make: accepting that they were meant to be husband and wife. "We need to figure this out," she whispered, determination in her weary voice.

Despite the melancholy mood that swept over Gracie as she headed to the apartment that she shared with Dillian on Turtle Creek, an upscale area in the Dallas area, she couldn't help but smile about the positives in her life. She had a parking spot at the fitness center that read "Owner Parking Only" for crying out loud. Her plan 'A' might have failed, but her plan 'B' gave her an abundance of blessings.

A nice luxury car, an apartment in one of the best neighborhoods and a booming business right in the heart of downtown Dallas, Gracie was a person of most people's dreams. She'd defied the odds—being an African American plus being a woman. Gracie had achieved a dream for many. Rubbing her thigh with her right hand, Gracie smiled as she thought about her blessings.

Gracie, you are beautiful, whole, and almost complete! What on earth are you stressing about? She reminded herself.

Reaching for her rearview mirror, she stared back at the brown distinctive eyes that were looking at her. She was a gorgeous individual that made a statement, be it in tights or a two-piece suit, her honey-colored skin rounded off her completeness whether she knew it or not.

As far as the gym, with her clientele growing at a rapid pace, she had already begun expanding her business ideas. Now she was focusing on opening another gym and even adding a small spa. That quest alone would make her one of the first young African-American women to venture into the fitness world in Dallas, twice over, operating and owning her dream.

Just thinking about the new plans made Gracie frown because Dillian had been number one on her list to run the spa. Now that their relationship was on pins and needles, she had a lot of rethinking to do.

As she pulled off the reconstructed and widened Highway 75, Gracie maneuvered through the narrow streets of her complex. Easing her custom-made champaign interior on champaign exterior Mercedes Benz C-class through the opened garage door, Gracie took off her sunglasses. She was shocked when she noticed the U-Haul truck parked in front of their condo.

Gracie reluctantly eased her body out of the driver's seat, forgetting to take the key out of the car's ignition.

Gracie pressed the strands of black lengthy hair that had fallen out of her ponytail back into place. Heading directly toward her boyfriend—turned fiancé months prior with the 2.5 carat engagement ring—Gracie had questions as Dillian continued his walk away from the rented truck.

She didn't know whether to scream or to cry, so instead, she did neither. Her voice steady, her eyes leveled, Gracie started. "Excuse me, Dillian, I'm sorry to bother you, but what on earth are you doing?"

With his six-foot-one-inch frame, Dillian halted with bags in tow and lowered them to the ground. Rubbing his slightly calloused and now empty hands profusely, Dillian was ashamed that Gracie had caught him in his escape.

"Gracie I thought you wouldn't be able to get away from the gym?" Dillian had no choice but to apologize in the awkward moment. "Look, I'm sorry, okay?"

As she searched for sincerity in Dillian's once honesty

filled eyes, Gracie could not believe that her well-groomed, black knight of a fiancé was walking away from her. "Sorry? Sorry for what? I thought we needed to talk, but I didn't think you meant talk about you moving out! Can you help me more clearly understand what's going on?"

Through her tears, Gracie took in the blurry images of Dillian's bags, the U-Haul truck, and then Dillian's face. She was beyond confused and her heart was breaking slowly. Dillian guided Gracie to the apartment by the elbow.

Dillian sat a despondent Gracie down on the couch in the living room while he took a seat on the sofa opposite her. He took her hands. Opening his mouth to speak, his words were in no hurry.

"I knew this was going to be hard," he muttered. "I thought about leaving a letter," he said, more to himself than to Gracie.

"Dillian?"

Dillian looked up into Gracie's heavy eyes, full of confusion and questions.

"Gracie I know you don't completely understand what is going on and I may look like a coward to you, but I need to leave. I have to go. I've put us in a situation that isn't good for either one of us."

"But . . . but Dillian, I don't understand. All relationships have rocky times. You don't talk to me when I'm here. What's going on?" Gracie reached out her hands, wanting to throw her arms around Dillian to let him know that things could get better, but he stopped her in mid-air.

Dillian sat back on the sofa and wished he could make this bad dream go away. No matter how many times he closed his eyes, reality was still present.

"I owe you an explanation. I know that." Dillian offered, "You just need to understand that I will give you one. Just not right now." Dillian lowered his head, taking Gracie out of his eyesight. It pained him to know that he was walking away from her—*the* woman of all women. She was close enough to perfection in his eyes, which made it more than painful to do what he had to do.

Not being able to control her shaking hands or the jumping of her legs, Gracie's attractive face was hidden behind her tears.

"What! You expect me to just let you go?" She looked down at her ring and fingered it, twirling it around her slender finger. "You put this ring on my finger, Dillian. What am I supposed to do, just let it go because you can't do it? Because you *won't* do it? Talk to me. Tell me something I don't know, because obviously I know nothing! Obviously I don't even know you!"

After taking in the questions, Dillian ran his hand over his stubble beard. "Just let me go. I'm dealing with a lot right now. Just let me go." Dillian walked back to Gracie to finish what he started. "I love you, Gracie. I love you with all my being. Please forgive me." Dillian bent down and placed a kiss on Gracie's left temple before leaving.

With her last bit of energy, Gracie curled up in the fetal position and cried. Her *what about me* questions would just have to be answered by her own instinct. She couldn't—and wouldn't—do anymore.

Although she wanted nothing more than to run after her "Mr. Right," Gracie had always told herself that if a man had enough guts to let her know that he didn't want her, she would be woman enough to accept it. She had seen, time and time again, women throwing themselves back into meaningless relationships all for the comfort. She had made it twenty-six years without throwing herself at a man, and she didn't plan on making herself a statistic yet.

Gracie was an only child and her parents were nearing seventy years in age. So she felt there was no way she could call them and put her burdens on them, but she needed to talk. The pain that bled inside her was too much to keep in. With a shaky hand, Gracie reached out and picked up the phone behind her on the end table and dialed her godparents' number instead.

"Hello, you've reached the Caleb's residence. Sorry we are unable to answer your call at this time. If you would briefly leave a detailed message, we will be sure to return your call promptly."

"Hello? Nancy? It's me, Gracie. I need you to call me when you get a chance. It's nothing life threatening, but I need to talk to you. I need to talk to someone." After hanging up the phone, Gracie decided against her own decision and picked up the telephone to call her parents as well.

After telling her mother that she would be driving down for the weekend, the cheer in her mother's voice almost made her think twice. All she wanted to do was to cry, and cry some more. Hiding her pain would be a difficult task if she chose to not let her parents in on her secret, which is exactly what she had planned to do.

Knowing that she needed the fresh air to clear her mind, she promised herself that she could fake the funk just enough to get some rest and strength at her parents'. Not being one to let her family down, Gracie kept a smile over the phone until the call ended. As soon as it did, she grabbed for the handmade throw at the end of the sofa and cried herself to sleep.

* * *

Gracie's eyes were almost sealed shut by the tears she had shed before she faded off into her miserable sleep. Kicking her legs to the side of the sofa to sit up, Gracie ran her hands across her face. She left her hair mangled and she questioned the lonely apartment. "How could he do this to me?" With no answer, she went into deep thought to see if she could answer her own question. "Just like he did, Gracie. Just like he did."

As she walked into the hallway restroom and gathered a towel to wash her face, nothing came to mind. Lathering the Dove soap and applying it to her soft, blemish-free face, every time she would think she found a reason why Dillian had "dissed" her, she came up with nothing.

She thought that maybe it was their lovemaking. She knew they had their spats about her wanting to be all lovey-dovey and him avoiding it all together. Knowing about the ongoing problems with his knees and the medication that he had to take daily, Gracie still wouldn't allow herself to believe that arthritis would break up their once happy union.

Knowing that it would be a while before she would completely get over or understand what had just happened in her life, Gracie regrouped, rinsed the soap from her now-fresh face, and disappeared into her master bedroom and packed.

A numb Gracie left Kendra a message on their private office line, letting Kendra know that she was taking the remainder of the day off. Since she was already off on weekends, she asked to be covered on Monday as well. She needed the time to air out some personal issues.

After loading her disheveled luggage into the car, Gracie went back in the apartment and tried to find the energy to straighten it up. With no avail, she decided to take a cold shower instead. She changed into nice black slacks and a thin beige cardigan sweater for the ride into Paris, Texas. Gracie was ready for fresh air.

In the car, Gracie gripped the steering wheel hard and took deep breaths. She counted to ten and pulled out of the driveway before slipping her sunglasses on. She needed them to cover her cried-out eyes. Thoughts of the last three hours passed her mind as she exhaled and pulled off.

How could she have been so naïve? She should have seen the breakup coming. But when should she have taken notice? It all happened overnight, it seemed. If only she could pinpoint the time when things had gone haywire, but would that change anything?

For the hour-and-thirty-minute ride, she chose to ride in silence to put her thoughts in order and pull herself together for the next phase in her life. All of her plans were now null and void, and she had no way of knowing where to pick up.

Maybe she could drown herself in her work, but what good would that do? There were only so many stairsteps and lightweight exercises one could do. She couldn't let herself be in denial. The itch that many women her age had, herself included, had just been scratched.

Her dreams of buying a house with Dillian, their wedding, and even the birth of their first child had been crossed off of her to-do list. But she hoped that wouldn't be a permanent thing. But how could all of her dreams come true at her age? She was getting older and too mature to start playing cat-and-mouse games with men. It would take her another two years or so before she could start a relationship and get to know someone. Gracie had a timeline, and it was off course.

With so many things to think about, especially how to let Kendra in on her embarrassing secret, she decided to push all of her mental let-downs to the back of her mind and put the pedal to the metal. Letting the air hold her problems for a while, Gracie drove in a trance and didn't become coherent until she saw the green building that had always let her know that she had arrived in P-town.

CHAPTER TWO

Knowing that she wouldn't get a signal on the ride up to the doctor's office, Kendra had waited until she passed the elevator's threshold to push send on her cellular phone. She waited until the conversation was almost finished before entering.

"Thank you so much, Patrick! I know Gracie will be happy that you can take over her classes while she is away. Okay, great! I'll talk to you when I get back to the gym. Thanks again." Letting out a sigh of relief, Kendra was happy to know that their old pal Patrick could come through for them. It wasn't hard to find a substitute for their aerobics classes, but it was hard to find the best.

Kendra waited in the short line to sign her name on the waiting list. When she arrived at the window, she made sure the nurse knew that she had an appointment.

"Yes, I'm here for a four o'clock appointment. Kendra Jackson."

"Yes, Ma'am, sign your name and we'll call you back in just a few."

"Thank you." Kendra turned her cell phone's ring to vibrate. It annoyed her when people with cell phones would leave them at high-volume rings in some of the most public places.

She wasn't watching where she was going, but she was listening. She could hear Dr. Shields on the other side of the glass that was still open for the next client to sign up. Dr. Shields was talking to a client about the importance of getting with a support group as the door opened. Kendra looked up and saw the doctor say good-bye to his patient. Kendra's mouth dropped. She jumped behind a wall before being noticed by Dr. Shields . . . or Dillian.

She found a vacant chair to sit in, behind the same wall that covered her from familiar eyes. Kendra thought before jumping to conclusions. She was aware that she always ran into someone she knew at Dr. Shields' office. He catered to mostly athletes. Because of his expertise, his practice was growing.

But still, at the words "support group", she thought of the problems that Dillian and Gracie had been having. Kendra couldn't dig fast enough to find her celly to call her best friend. Right as she was about to push the send key to connect her call, her name was called for her appointment.

After the nurse had done all the basics: blood pressure and weight and height checks, Kendra sat on the cold vinyl table and settled in as comfortable as she could with the thin-as-snow, paper gown she had changed into. Her mind played back to the earlier scene in the waiting room. With one swoop, Kendra jumped down off of the table to reach for her cell phone. Once again, she was knocked off course as Dr. Shields entered the room, ready for their visit.

Noticing Kendra shuffling between the chair in the corner and the examination table, the doctor took a jab. "Oh Miss Jackson, did you need extra time? I can go to the next room and see the next patient if you need me to."

"Ohhh, no you don't!" Kendra joked as she put her phone back in her purse. Holding the behind of her gown, Kendra eased herself back into place on the table. "I already waited a lifetime for you to begin with, and you of all people know I don't have that kind of time."

"Well, look at you! I'm slow now, huh? Oh okay, let me let you wait just a little longer." Dr. Shields turned, acting as though he would leave the room.

"Jokes! They're all jokes, Doc. You know I'm only kidding."

"That's what I thought," he reassured her with a slight laugh. "So how has it all been going for you, Kendra?" the doctor asked as he placed the chart on the counter.

"Dr. Shields?" With her voice reaching lower octaves, Kendra gave her doctor a glare from the corners of her eyes.

"Right, I forgot," the young, successful doctor who resembled the actor Hill Harper responded as he scooted his wheeled stool over to his patient. "But I can't help but try. I know you don't like the mushy side of my profession. It's not all books you know. I do care about my patients, Miss Jackson."

"I don't doubt it . . . I'm just not there yet. But just to let you off the hook. All's well."

Placing his stethoscope earbuds in both ear, Dr. Shields listened to Kendra's breathing. After giving her different breathing techniques, Dr. Shields continued his examination, making her do different stretches to pull muscles in her back. Concluding his short examination, Dr. Shields charted and stood up. He walked over to the cabinet where the room supplies were housed and slipped on the large, non-powder gloves.

"Oh! Umm. What are you doing with those gloves, Doc?"

With a needle in his gloved hand, Dr. Shields turned to face a frightened Kendra. "Now, Kendra, you want new vitamins right?" She nodded affirmatively. "Well, I have to make sure there are no negative reactions with the other medications your primary doctor already has you on before I can go prescribing different vitamins or medicines."

Unhappy with the answer, Kendra reluctantly agreed to the blood draw. She didn't know for sure, but her usual vitamins weren't working like they used to. For the last couple of weeks, she had been battling a cold that kept her coughing and sniffling, and she had less energy.

As Dr. Shields placed the used needle in the red biohazard container, Kendra thought it would be a good time to answer her questions out about Dillian.

"I thought I saw Dillian leaving here when I first got in."

With his back to his long-time patient, Dr. Shields responded. "Yes, that was Dillian. Speaking of him, how is Gracie? Tell her to come on in if she needs her chiropractic touch-up for the year. That girl's a hard worker."

"Yes she is. And I definitely will do." During the friendly conversation, Kendra wanted so much to probe more into Dillian's "special treatment," but she didn't want to put her doctor on the spot.

As he held the door open to leave, Dr. Shields reminded Kendra that he would call in a prescription for her as soon as he received her results.

"You don't have to come back in. If you'll just leave your pharmacist's number at the front, that will be all."

"Okay. Sounds like a plan. I actually think Sandra has my pharmacy's number."

"Good. Well, just leave my money at the front and be on your way."

They shared a final laugh. Kendra got up from the table and dressed to leave.

CHAPTER THREE

A visit to Paris was just what Gracie needed to get away from the city, even if it wasn't the city that was bothering her; just the people in it. She needed to feel loved, and she was sure to receive all the love she needed from her parents.

She glided down the graveled back roads that were familiar, yet new. Gracie loved the town where she could easily feel at home. Things had changed, but not majorly. A few new high schools had been built, but the old stomping ground, Paris High, where Gracie was voted most athletic, was still standing strong.

As she drove through the town en route to her parent's home, Gracie decided to pass by some of the old spots and reminisce. She drove the pass-through road that held the same skating rink where she had plenty of birthday parties. She smiled as she watched a young boy skate past the security guard, in an attempt to leave the skating grounds with rented skates.

She turned onto the street that was not where she'd grown up. It was the new house that her parents had bought a few years back. Gracie thought about when her parents prepared her for a world that was much bigger than Paris. They knew that Dallas was one place that Gracie would eventually touch.

They themselves went down the same path, leaving Paris at an early age only to return when they were ready to settle peacefully. Her parents were young and in love. They had stayed together for more than fifty-five years. They rarely had any conflicts. They both credited waiting for love—instead of looking for it—for their longevity.

They were in total awe of one another. In their middle adult years when people asked if they had ever thought about or wanted children, they honestly said no, in a mutual agreement. They were best friends and were too afraid to hinder their closeness. However, after many happy and content years together, Mrs. Gregory—at the age of forty—woke up one morning and felt like she had more to give the world. When she talked to her husband, Jacob, about her feelings, he felt they had more to offer as well. And indeed they had.

Two years later, Gracie was conceived and born into a loving household that spoiled her beyond compare. Since she had older parents, growing up could have been hard for her in a big city. But since she was in the country, it didn't make a world of difference. Her parents stayed and raised Gracie in Paris because they were more grounded there.

They were well known because of their neighborhood store. Since Paris was more like a giant neighborhood than a town, things went smoothly. Smooth enough for her to one day consider moving back, but only at a resting age, like her parents.

As Gracie parked her car in front of her parents' home, she noticed a message on her two-way. Gracie read the message from Kendra: *CALL ME NOW*. Instead of replying to it, she decided to turn off her pager and her cell phone and begin her visit.

Sitting out front of her parents' five-year-old home, honking the horn, Gracie was glad to know that her folks were still up and about, able to walk fast, if not run out to the car and help her with her luggage. They gave her inspiration and good genes to look forward to when it was her time to wait for kids to return back home.

Gracie had no intentions of laying everything on the table for her parents to deal with. They had become very fond of Dillian, as she had over the years, and they would only be waiting to hear good news. Plus, bad news would make them think that was the only reason she had come home. She hated to admit it to herself, but if things had been lovely for her and Dillian, she wouldn't be visiting her parents until the holidays rolled around.

"Hey, girlie! Catherine, come on and look who's outside trying to pull her own weight and then some!" Yelling back for his wife to make her way outside, Jacob let out a tickled laugh as he called his only daughter by her nickname.

"Hey, Daddy!" Gracie grinned from ear to ear. Just looking into her father's eyes, she could feel his love. At that moment, she felt that everything would always be okay. "Can you help me?"

Walking closer to his daughter's car, Jacob Gregory gave her a quick kiss on the cheek and took her bags from her. He had been an athletic man back in his day, and his stories had been the motivation for Gracie as she started on her own athletic journey. She couldn't recall a time that her father wasn't in the stands cheering her on. Cheering her up after a not-so-good track meet meant a ride in his vintage Mustang with her driving.

Finally making her way outdoors to her family, Mrs. Gregory was a settled-in, older, and satisfied woman. With just a little bit of aging around her eyes, Mrs. Gregory was surely the mirror that Gracie would look into when she reached that age.

Attempting to run with her hands in the air, Mrs. Gregory was overjoyed.

"There's my baby. Aw, come give your mama a kiss."

Pretending that she wasn't going to give away any kisses to her mother, Gracie knew the fly swatter in her mother's hand would land on her behind. As it did.

"Girl, don't think you're too big for no whooping." Embracing her daughter, Mrs. Gregory's heart was always big when it came to Gracie. Gracie was her pride and joy. Her name was originally supposed to be Elizabeth. Catherine said once she delivered her baby girl, it was like God's grace had brought her through the hard delivery. Thus, she named the child Gracie.

"Come on in here and get you something to eat," her father said. "I know you probably ain't eating nothing but berries and fruits. Thinking you're Ms. Aerobics and all." Mr. Gregory would always suggest that Gracie add a little more to her slender frame.

"Ha, ha. That's very funny, Daddy. Just 'cause you like all of this," Gracie said, grabbing at her mother's butt, "doesn't mean that everyone does." Gracie received a pinch as her mother caught her wrist before she could jerk her hands away.

"Alright now! Jake, go ahead and put that stuff in the backroom while me and Gracie go finish dinner."

"Uh, Ma! I didn't come down here to cook. I came to eat," Gracie said as she took off the top layer of her cardigan.

The eye was all she had to give Gracie to let her know who the parent was and always would be. "I wasn't expecting you until the holidays," her mother continued as she halted while wiping her hands on her apron. "What brought you this way?"

Hoping that her mother would change her mind about making her help with dinner, Gracie suppressed the pressure with her mother's question.

"Nothing. I just wanted to come home for the weekend." She scooped up a spoonful of homemade mashed potatoes.

"So you don't say, huh?" Pass me that black pepper from the table. How's the business coming along?" She stopped what she was doing and looked up every once and a while. Mrs. Gregory wanted to make sure she looked into her only daughter's eyes for the truth.

"It's doing fine, and Kendra sends her love."

"Tell her we said hi. What about Dillian? What's he up to?" With her back to her daughter as she cut potatoes around the roast, Mrs. Gregory arched her eyebrows in secret to see if the truth would be revealed.

"Uh, Dillian's fine. You need any help?"

"No, hun, I'm fine. And why didn't he come down with you?"

Gracie's mind raced. She tried to think as fast as she could for something to say. She didn't want to lie to her mother, but she didn't want her mother to worry about her either. "He couldn't get out of his training classes. Business is steadily booming for him, too. Did I tell you? Ever since he appeared on *Morning Texas*, he's been getting all kinds of offers from clients trying to get their swoll' on."

"Humph. That's good. I think you did mention something to me about that. That's real good."

"Other than that, everything has been the same."

Gracie made her way to the refrigerator with a bowl in tow. She knew her parents always kept old-fashioned vanilla ice cream for dessert. For once, she wasn't going to think about her diet, health, wealth, or anything that usually controlled her life. She just wanted to sulk in her secret pain.

Just as Gracie dropped the last scoopful into her awaiting bowl, Mrs. Gregory dropped her own bomb.

"Really? Well, I wonder why you don't have on your engagement ring."

Busted! There was no way of getting around the ring. Dropping her spoon in her bowl full of ice cream, Gracie dropped her head and walked to the table. With her head down and both forearms on the kitchen table, she closed her eyes. She didn't notice her father come into the kitchen or her mother swat him away so that they could have personal time.

Gracie knew that she couldn't hide her real reason for leaving Dallas any longer. But she did have the option of telling the whole story or telling a partial truth. She was too embarrassed to let her mother know that Dillian had walked out on her.

In her mother's eyes and in her own, Gracie was a beautiful woman. She had smooth skin and shoulder-length hair that she mostly kept in ponytails on her workings days. She had the body that most women worked for desperately. No fat nor cellulite to be found on her body, Gracie adopted the love of taking care of her physical being at a young age and cared about staying in shape for herself, first and foremost. Being eye candy for most men wasn't a big disappointment either. Though she had what most people coveted, Gracie felt she obviously didn't have enough to hold onto a man. She didn't know how she was going to tell her mother, but she had to start somewhere.

"I don't have the ring on, because . . ." Gracie choked on her words.

Catherine walked closer to Gracie and took a seat beside her. "Gracie, I'm your mother. If you need to talk about something, go ahead, baby."

"I don't have the ring on because I don't think there will be a wedding. Dillian and I have broken up." There was no way she could let it all out.

"Oh Gracie, honey. I'm sorry. You should have told me. I may be getting old, but I'm still your mother."

With tears in her eyes, Gracie wished she could lay all of her new problems on the line with her mother, but she knew she couldn't. The pain of being walked out on was too much to share. Most people wouldn't understand where she was coming from. Some might even say that she was taking the breakup too hard. But when you're good friends with the love of your life and things dwindle and then eventually die, there's more where the tears come from.

"Thank you, Mama. I should have known I could talk to you about anything. Thank you for listening."

"No problem. Let me refill your bowl for you; get you some fresh ice cream. We're not through yet." Getting up from the small framed kitchen table, Mrs. Gregory grabbed for the bowl of melted ice cream. Singing a little tune of *"Precious Lord"* on her short trip, she refilled her daughter's bowl. She wiped her wet hands on her apron and sat back down.

With a new bowl of ice cream in front of her, Gracie listened to her mother talk of love, fear, and time. "Gracie, love comes and goes through people who don't understand what they have until it's gone, at times. The fear of love is so strong in men, you know, because they are not often taught that love can be a beautiful thing. They just don't know or choose not to believe

that love can be fulfilling and rewarding." She continued. "Above all, Gracie, don't forget you have time.
You're young, beautiful, and healthy. Your dreams may
have been postponed, but when the end result comes,
you'll have more to offer. Our time is not the same as
God's time. I like to think of it as Him giving us time to
make more room for the abundant blessings we'll have
to receive."

Gracie looked into her mother's eyes and let out a
sigh of relief. She ate her ice cream as she thought
about her future. Giving herself a personal pep talk
while her mother continued, she dug deep inside of her
being and knew she had to look for the positive in a
negative situation. Not wanting to run after Dillian to
make things better, Gracie was ready to heal and
move forward in whatever direction her future went.
Alone.

They sat a little longer than they had planned.
Mrs. Gregory got a bowl and filled it to the rim with ice
cream as she had done for Gracie. As if she'd heard her
daughter's thoughts, Mrs. Gregory wanted to make
sure her daughter knew she was loved.

"You are not alone you know. Me and your father
adore you. Why do you think we always trying to get
you down here with us?" She shared in a laugh with
her daughter. "Whenever your husband finds you,
Gracie, he will indeed be blessed with a jewel. Keep
living for God, baby."

Shaking her head, Gracie wouldn't allow any more
tears to be shed. She would enjoy her stay at her parents', gather strength, and start on her life alone.

CHAPTER FOUR

By Sunday morning, Gracie's weekend stay at her parents' was about over. She debated whether to hit Interstate 30 and head back to Dallas or visit a little longer with her family. She decided to stay until Wednesday. She'd contact Kendra to give her the rundown about her absence and make sure she was covered with her classes.

When Kendra heard Gracie's voice over the phone, she let out a loud whoosh.

"Well it's about time!" Kendra complained. "Where in the heck have you been? I've been calling and two-way paging you all weekend, girl!"

"Calm down, Ken," Gracie said. "I'm sorry. I know I should have called you, but I was upset."

Within seconds, Gracie had spilled the entire story to Kendra, and her heart felt better for doing so.

"Gracie, I am really sorry to hear about the breakup, but didn't you think it was coming?"

"Yeah, but even so, I had never imagined it would be so blatant and unresolved. I'm still taken aback by the whole ordeal." Feeling tears form, Gracie quickly closed her eyes and attempted to suppress them.

"And as you should be, girl! Well, you have nothing to worry about. Anytime you need to talk, I'm here for you. Not only are you my best friend, I'm your best friend too. Don't you forget that, okay?"

"Thanks, girl."

"No problem. And while we're on the subject of Dillian, I went to Dr. Shield's on Friday and I saw him there."

"Dillian?"

"Yes, ma'am." Kendra answered in a swayed response.

Sitting with her manicured nail at the tip of her lip, Gracie couldn't remember if Dillian had a doctor's appointment or not.

"I wonder if his knee is bothering him again. You know it's been bothering him for a while. I know it was about three weeks ago, and Dr. Shield's had to give him a shot. Maybe that's why he was there."

"I don't know." Taking a seat on the edge of her bed, Kendra hesitated putting her pantyhose on so that she could tell Gracie the remainder of what she heard. "He wasn't limping or anything, but I did hear the doctor mention joining a support group."

"A support group? That's weird. Maybe he meant talking to people with chronic arthritis or something. Oh well, that no longer involves me," Gracie responded, wondering if there could be more to Dillian's story than what he was saying.

"Yeah, maybe you're right. It is a small world anyway, and you know how I get stuff twisted."

"Well, whatever the case, good looking out for me." Gracie made sure her worry didn't show through the phone to Kendra. "Girl, I better go ahead and get off this phone. You know my momma will start thinking I'm trying to avoid church. Thanks for taking care of things. You're a sweetheart!"

"That's what friends are for. I need to finish getting ready for church too. I'll see you when you get back."

"Whaaaat? You're going to church? Someone must have put fire to your behind!" Gracie said while laughing.

"Ha, ha. Very funny. Actually, one of my clients invited me, so I said I'd check it out."

"Oh, okay. Oh, Ken! Why did you go to see the doctor anyway?"

"Girl, uh, nothing. I just had my follow-up with Dr. Shields on my back from the car wreck. And you know I had that hacking cold. He was supposed to give me a new vitamin."

"Hmm. Oh, okay. I almost forgot about the terrible cough you had that even made my chest hurt." They shared a final laugh. "Okay, well I'll talk to you later then . . . bye."

Gracie gathered her clothes and personal items. She wanted to put her mind at ease, wondering whether Dillian was ill or not. Knowing that she was pressed for time, Gracie fought to put her thoughts to the back of her mind and God to the front of her heart in preparation for church.

When Gracie arrived at the Holiness Church, she felt refreshed before even setting foot in the front door. She didn't get that rush at some of the big churches in Dallas.

There were 500 members and about 200 members came each Sunday. They were all "Rock Danieling" in unison when the Gregorys walked through the chapel doors.

Immediately, Gracie joined in with praise and worship, taking her problems to the altar when the prayer line was called. Like most people who sit on the pews with heavy burdens, Gracie didn't care who thought what. She had no qualms about getting extra prayer any time she felt she needed it.

At the altar, Gracie felt guilty. Knowing that she should have prayed for her and Dillian's relationship sooner, she asked for God's forgiveness. At the front of the church, she knew she would have to let all the baggage go and start fresh . . . and that's what she did.

"Yes, yes, yes Lord!" Gracie cried out and thanked the Lord for keeping her. Gracie asked for strength for her personal trials that only God could help her with. Tears rushed down her face and her voice cried out loudly, Gracie purged her heart. Repenting to the Lord for seen and unseen mistakes on her part, Gracie thanked the Lord for loving her through her mistakes.

She felt fresh from the renewing of her spirit. Mother Humphrey, a missionary at the church, helped Gracie up. Gracie cried out to the Lord and knew that all would be well. "Thank the Lord. Thank Him. He's worthy to be praised! Thank you, Lord! Thank you, Lord!"

With her all being poured out to the Lord, Gracie knew it was going to take more than just crying out at the altar. She was going to have to accept and believe that God would help her through her tribulations. Accepting prayer and asking God to help her pull through, Gracie, returned to her seat, praising God. Before Gracie could sit down, her mother rose and hugged her, giving her the motherly love that Gracie so desperately needed.

Other than her heart, Gracie had no idea there was more in her life that could possibly be broken. Knowing that her problems were out of her hands, she worshipped and praised the Lord for fixing her problems even though she knew she didn't deserve it.

When Wednesday rolled around, Gracie still wasn't ready to leave but she knew that she had a business to get back to and a life to continue.

Gracie walked into the den where her parents were sitting watching talk shows, and took a seat on the vacant sofa.

"I'm about to head out," Gracie said. "I got the plate out of the microwave you fixed for me, Momma. Thank you."

"Girlie, don't be taking my food out of my mouth," Jacob said with a stern expression on his face. "You're the one with the big bucks. Just leave a ten spot on your way out." His grimace vanished into a smile, and he laughed.

"I wish I would leave a spot of anything!" Gracie had a smirk on her face as she joked with her father. The three of them burst into laughter.

Gracie walked to the mantle and looked at old pictures of which her parents had been so proud throughout the years. Gracie couldn't believe some of the old styles that she had gone through.

"Oh my goodness, look at me with this mushroom hairdo. I look a hot mess!" Gracie stopped when she came to one particular picture. "Momma, are you going to ever take down this picture of me and Marcus?"

"Let my picture alone! You leave my Marcus where he belongs. Oh, did I tell you he came by not too long ago when he came down to visit his folks?" Catherine cut her eyes and gave a flirty smile, sounding as though she was ready to gossip.

"Of course you did, Momma. Every time you find something out about Marcus, you call and let me know. Don't act like you don't."

"Oh," Mrs. Gregory sighed guiltily.

Jacob stood and moved his wife and daughter out of the way of the television. "Excuse me," he said. "Y'all need to move." He was missing the most important part of the talk show . . . the fight.

"Sorry, Daddy."

"That's okay. It's a repeat anyway. But yeah, old Marcus came by here and asked about you and everything." He wanted to continue with the gossip. "I can't believe you two don't ever run into each other up yonder."

Gracie closed her eyes and shook her head in disbelief at her father for his age-old remarks, always easing Marcus into conversations. Gracie walked into the kitchen, grabbed other items, and prepared to leave. "Uh, oh. It's time for me to go. That was high school, Daddy. Let it go!"

She said her goodbyes and reassured her parents that she would call and let them know when she made it home. Gracie was headed back to her condo to be alone.

Making sure that all of her belongings were intact, Gracie sat for a second in her car, and put all of her thoughts out on the table. She knew that times would be rough with her new single life, but she also knew that she had the strength from within to stand through the pain. With her newfound strength from the altar, Gracie cranked her car, put the gear in drive, and looked forward to moving on.

Again, without music, Gracie headed down the familiar streets until she hit the highway. This time she didn't wear her sunglasses so that she could see just where she was headed.

CHAPTER FIVE

Gracie did what many women did when they wanted to avoid a broken heart: she filled her life with work, work, and more work. Pouring all of her energy into the gym, Gracie added an extra class a day to her schedule, and even considered going forward with her plans to open Full of Grace Fitness Gym II.

Though Gracie's mind was racing with thoughts of contractors, sites, amenities and more, she couldn't shake one non-work related detail from her mind . . . Marcus.

There was something about seeing the pictures of her and Marcus that had Gracie's *what ifs* spinning faster than the wheels on her car on the way back from Paris. Since then, he had been on her mind. While she was going through her fresh breakup with Dillian, she couldn't help but think about her and Marcus's breakup close to five years earlier.

At eighteen, the responsibilities of a relationship were more than she and Marcus had bargained for. They said "I love you" faster than their actual bond developed. They didn't realize until weeks, months, even years later that it takes work to create a successful partnership.

The one saving grace about the breakup was that the two decided to remain on speaking terms; however, they never saw each other to have the chance to speak.

Marcus shocked Gracie when he proposed that they rekindle their flame if by the age twenty-five, they hadn't walked down the aisle of holy matrimony. Thinking back about the perfect match she thought she had with Dillian, Gracie wondered if Marcus had found his.

Age twenty-five had come and gone by a year and a few months. The idea that had once been so clear was now just an easy memory about their young relationship. *There was no way he could have really meant that.* Now that the years had passed by, she would never know.

Gracie learned from her caring parents that Marcus lived in Houston and was an assistant football coach at one of the most popular universities. Despite this information and her constant thoughts of Marcus, Gracie thought it was best to let go of the far-off fairy tale. She didn't know why she had suddenly chosen to let Marcus enter her daydreams, but she couldn't get him out. Trying her best to do something other than think about Marcus, she penciled in her new appointment with a well-known contractor for the following day.

"Now we have five, four, three . . ." As Gracie counted down to the end of another high-powered aerobic class, she smirked at the exhausted faces of her pupils. A few of them fell to the floor.

"That's all for today, class," Gracie said. "Sorry for

the hard workout, but hey, that's what you pay me for, right?" Gracie yanked her headset off and joined in with the limp laughter of her class.

Later, in the foyer—which resembled the lobby of a hotel with its open area, high ceilings, and elegant decorum—Gracie sat behind the front desk, which had a full view of the entrance with the young receptionist.

"Has Kendra come out of class yet?" she asked.

"Uh, yes, Ms. Gregory," Latriece replied. She looked over her schedule book. "You just missed her by five minutes actually. She said she had to run a quick errand but would return shortly."

"Dang." Gracie sighed. "I needed to let her know about the appointment tomorrow." Gracie snatched up her two-way pager and punched in her request for Kendra to clear her schedule for the latter part of the next day. Gracie's head was down when a sports utility vehicle pulled up at the drop off point.

"Whew!" Latriece exclaimed. "I wonder who's rolling in the big body."

"Girl, if you don't act like those . . ." Gracie cut herself off before she said that Latriece reminded her of those video honeys who fawned over men's rides. Gracie looked up and felt her body implode when she saw who the "big body" belonged to.

Coming from the back of the building where the classes were held, Michelle said her goodbyes. "See you on Thursday, Gracie. Take it easy."

Shaken out of her zombie trance, Gracie Gregory barely got a goodbye out to the young lawyer who had recently started taking her class.

"Uh, oh. Bye, Michelle. See you then." She waved to her new client and watched as Michelle waited on the passenger side of the truck as the driver finished his walk around the truck and held open the door for her. The tall, well-built gentleman was none other than Marcus Jeffries.

She thought she would faint! Gracie couldn't walk down the hall and into her office fast enough to call her mother and tell her who she had just seen.

"Momma! Oh my goodness. You won't believe who I just saw."

"What? A ghost I guess by the way you sound," Catherine said as she let out a laugh. She cleared her throat and took on a serious tone for Gracie's sake. "You sound all excited. Who'd you see, baby?"

"Marcus! Can you believe it? I mean, I had been thinking about him ever since I saw the picture of us, and he just appears! Oh my goodness."

"Really? What did you say to him? Where you see him at?" Half-way covering the phone with her hand, Catherine told Jacob who Gracie had seen. "She saw Marcus."

"He didn't see me, well, we didn't see each other, I mean. Well, I think his girlfriend is in one of my classes," Gracie finally managed to stammer out.

"Uh, oh."

"Uh, oh, what?"

"Nothing. I wonder if it's the girl he brought down here with him to meet his folks. How does she look?"

After a brief description, Gracie's excitement was already dwindling. However, she didn't know how, but she was determined to get information on Marcus, even if it had to be through his girlfriend, Michelle.

CHAPTER SIX

Kendra stopped writing in her palm pilot and sat still. She couldn't believe what Gracie was telling her.

"So, is this the same Marcus that I missed by three months, two days, and eleven hours?" Gracie had broken off her relationship with Marcus before she and Kendra met and became dorm mates.

"Yeppers. That's the one."

Kendra readjusted the straw in her cold drink that she had picked up on her way back to work and took a sip. "Dang, and I just had to run to the drug store. You know I would have gotten you hooked up!"

Kendra wasn't one for sitting around mourning over a man for too long. She believed in living and living a little more; part of the reason why she wished she had been there when Gracie saw Marcus. There was no doubt she would have gotten his attention.

"So you think he and Miss Prissy have something going on?"

Gracie shook her head, amused at her best friend.

She was afraid to give too much information to Kendra. She knew Kendra had a way of doing a lot of checking up on people and would do the same to Marcus. Even though she was a real "sista" at heart, looking at her outer appearance, one would think that Kendra herself was prissy because of her beauty.

"Well, I think so," Gracie answered while resting on the office's sofa. "From the description my momma gave me, it's her. The girlfriend. If not more."

"Well, we are just going to have to get the point across to old Marcus that the name on the building belongs to you." Gracie opened her mouth to protest, but Kendra continued. "Hmmm, what about having a *Bring Your Partner to Workout* day?"

They looked at each other for two seconds with deadpan expressions before kneeling over in laughter.

"You gonna have that girl trying to kill me," Gracie said. "She'll think I'm trying to steal her man right from under her nose."

She thought it would be a good idea to just sever all ties with Marcus when they broke up, so Gracie made her parents promise to not let him in on her life at any level. She thought she wouldn't want any surprise visits or phone calls from him, but now she wished he knew that it was her gym. She secretly regretted keeping her success away from Marcus.

Kendra shrugged. "Well, it's a thought. Sleep on it. It'll be a good idea."

"You're crazy!" Although she knew it was a crazy idea, Gracie gave it a thought.

Gracie got up from the sofa and walked over to her desk phone to check her messages at home. She already knew there wouldn't be important messages, but she liked to keep herself amused.

"We are calling concerning an important issue. This message is for a G. Gregory. Would you please contact the Human and . . ."

"Dang it!" That automatic message had been left on her home voicemail every day for more than two weeks, Gracie quickly pressed the number three key in the middle of the greeting to delete it. "I'm so sick of this crazy automated message in my inbox everyday."

Kendra looked up from her her palm pilot. "Girl, shoot. You never know. You could have won a romantic get-away to the Bahamas. You better listen next time."

"Whatever! With the luck I have, I don't think so. Who would I take anyway?"

"Uh, excuse me? You're looking at your romantic date right here," pointing to herself.

Shortly after, Gracie left their joint office and left Kendra alone in the spacious area. Kendra laid on the sofa and readied herself for her favorite mid-day television show to hit the screen. She was caught off guard when her personal cell phone rang. She usually got calls on her business cellular phone during the day. Kendra made her way to her desk and retrieved the call.

"Hello?" she answered as she tried to identify the number on the caller ID.

"Hey there . . . Kendra?"

"Yes," she responded as she sat down in the swivel chair. "Who's calling?"

Starting the conversation with a slight chuckle, Dr. Shields eased Kendra's worries. "You mean you don't know the voice of the person that charges you an arm and a leg for a good stretch? Dr. Shields here."

"Ha! Hey there! You can say that again. Are you calling me to give me a refund?"

"Not at all." He laughed again. "Listen, I wanted to check and see how the vitamins are working for you. Any side effects?"

"Hmm, no. Not that I've really been keeping track, but I believe everything is up to par."

"Great. Hey, but can you do me a favor? I need to talk to you about some things, but I can't really discuss them over the phone. Do you think you can come in?"

"Uh. Well. I guess if you need to talk to me, I'll have to make time. Is everything okay?"

Without answering her question, Dr. Shields let it be known that he would pencil her in for that afternoon. "I'll see you when you get here."

After she hung up, Kendra called Gracie, leaving a message that she would be out for the remainder of her break and would be back in the afternoon. Kendra got ready for her appointment with Dr. Shields. She knew that he was more than her doctor, but a friend. She already knew what he needed to talk to her about. It was something that she had been putting off talking to him about, but now it was time.

After exhausting herself at work, Gracie headed home and drew herself a long hot bath in her whirlpool tub. As the water caressed her skin, Gracie felt silly for thinking about moving out of the apartment. Despite those painful memories of Dillion, she realized the level of comfort the apartment brought to her. Gracie abandoned all her intentions of running away from her home.

After her bath, all Gracie could think about was climbing into her bed and drifting off into a deep sleep. That was what she always did after a hot soaking bath. Fearing she would oversleep, Gracie set her alarm clock thirty minutes early and passed out into the comfort of her bed.

Sleep came easily to Gracie. At least for four hours anyway. But almost in a flash, her sweet dreams turned in a familiar nightmare. The nightmare woke her up in a cold sweat and made Gracie sit up in her bed, with her breaths coming fast and hard as she tried to remember the face she had seen in her sleep.

"What is this about?" Gracie moaned as her mind spun, trying to figure out what the dream could mean.

The dream started like it always did. At the beginning of her relationship with Dillian, a relationship she thought was sturdy and loving. The sweetness of their love quickly faded, replaced by rough spots where the pair were hardly talking to one another. Dillian turned and walked away from Gracie, and she found herself running, trying to catch up with him, wanting to know why things went the way they had.

Gracie finally reached Dillian while he jogged on an outside track. She tapped his shoulder. Her face scrunched up in confusion when Dillian turned to face her. She could have sworn it was him; she knew his backside from anywhere, but the face didn't belong to Dillian. He'd somehow aged beyond his years.

Dillian opened his mouth but no words came out. Gracie watched his movements. His hands reached out and his eyes were wet. She felt that he was trying to say he was sorry. Over and over he motioned his apology. Gracie stood, confused and distraught, as Dillian backed away from her. His face was apologetic and tears of blood fell from his red eyes. Gracie screamed and begged for him to come back to her, but Dillian disappeared into a thick, gray fog, with the word 'sorry' echoing through the fog, scaring Gracie awake.

Gracie crawled from under her blankets and dangled her legs over the edge of her king-sized bed. She reached for her pager and texted Dillian her plea for him to respond. Her gut told her that she would get no response, but she would never know if she didn't try.

She just wanted the reason. Why did he leave? Why didn't he talk to her? Why didn't he give their relationship a chance? Gracie believed her dream was telling her a little more than she had known. Why else would Dillian spend so much money on her engagement ring and all of a sudden disappear into thin air? Something went wrong with Dillian, and Gracie had no idea what. She couldn't just let it go.

After drifting back to sleep, hours later, Gracie opened her eyes and found her head on the pillow and the pager still clutched in her hand. She wasn't surprised to find only one message: the weather watcher. She sighed heavily and scrolled to see how the day's weather would be. She got up to start her day.

CHAPTER SEVEN

Spring had sprung and summer was gone. Fall had arrived. With Thanksgiving quickly approaching, Gracie debated on going out on a whim and trying something she had never tried before: braids.

"Girl I'm telling you," Kendra said, "you're really going to like them. You said you were tired of doing your hair yourself, so go ahead and get the micros. If you don't like them, I'll reimburse you with half of the cost."

"I don't know. You know braids really aren't my forté. How about you reimburse me with time to take them down if I don't like them? If so, it's a deal."

"Well? Shoot! You got it."

Outside of the beauty salon, they shook on the deal and walked inside and got comfortable.

Kendra finished her treatments twenty minutes before Gracie and went to a nearby coffeehouse to get white mochas. She felt she needed something in her hands when she told Gracie about what happened when she had gone to the club and bumped into Dillian. Back in the salon, Kendra saw Gracie. Her braids looked fabulous.

"Oh my goodness!" Kendra squealed. "You look great, Gracie! Just let me know now, do I owe you?"

"Of course not." Gracie swung her head, showing off her braids. She placed a kiss on Kendra's cheek and grabbed for a mocha. "Girl, I owe you. Now give me my drink!"

As the pair walked down the sidewalk, Gracie playfully bumped shoulders with Kendra.

"In all honesty, Ken," Gracie began, "you are a real good friend and I just want you to know that I appreciate all of your friendly love."

"Aw girl. Now you know it's nothing but a thang!" Kendra leaned in to give Gracie a shoulder-to-shoulder hug. "I mean, even when you showed up at my house at midnight crying over spoiled milk and I wanted to slap some sense into you, I couldn't turn my back on you if I wanted to. You're my friend." Laughter filled the air.

When it came time to tell Gracie about seeing Dillian out on the town days prior, Kendra still couldn't find the words. At first, she didn't want to even bring Dillian's name up, but she figured Gracie needed to know, at least to stop her worries. When she tried to open her mouth to get the conversation started, a tall, handsome, copper-skinned younger man closed in the space in front of the two ladies.

"What's up, Kendra?" he asked.

Kendra, turned to look nervously at Gracie, then at the man. She stumbled over her words before she found them.

"Uh. Oh. Hey, T. What are you doing here? This is . . ."

"Shhh, Nothing really," he responded to Kendra in a lazy tone before she finished Gracie's introduction.

"Hey, what's up," he nodded to acknowledge Gracie. "Say, I was trying to make sure you made it home aiight that night, but you didn't answer . . . when we gon' hook up again? You trying to stay away from a brother?"

"Now you know better. You have one of my cards right?" Kendra asked with her eyes stretched extra-wide. She hoped that Gracie wouldn't read in between the lines.

"Yep, you know I do."

"Okay. Give me a call and I'll see when I can schedule you in."

"Cool," he said as he bent down and kissed her clammy cheek.

Kendra and Gracie walked in silence until they reached the exit door. Gracie wanted to ask about the man and the silent kiss, but she knew that Kendra did personal sessions on the side and just figured the young man wanted to be penciled in for a workout.

Kendra kept quiet as the two made their way from Stonebriar Mall to Gracie's apartment. Once there, Kendra could not hold her tongue any longer. If she waited, she feared she would never speak.

Once they were settled in Gracie's condo and all of their purchases had been looked over and compared, Kendra knew it was time to let Gracie in on what she had seen. As Gracie brought tea from the kitchen, Kendra took the cup from her long time friend. She was ready.

She took one sip before she placed her cup on the table. Kendra turned to Gracie to start the conversation.

"Gracie, you know how we have always told each other that if the other ever knew anything about our boyfriend, we would want to know?"

"Yeah, of course I remember," Gracie said as she took a sip of her steaming tea. "Why?" She gave Kendra her full attention as she wondered where the conversation was heading, although she had a good idea.

She had been comfortable on the sofa. But now it was uncomfortable, so Kendra shifted back and forth in her seat.

"Do you want to know, even if it's an ex-boyfriend?"

Suddenly, sensing that Kendra had something of importance to share with her about Dillian, Gracie grabbed both of their full cups of tea and went to the kitchen where she disposed of the drinks.

No matter what, Kendra knew there was no turning back and knew she had to continue. "Gracie, are you going to come out here or what?" she asked the wall that was between the kitchen and living area where Kendra sat.

Walking back into the living area, Gracie was as ready as she was going to be. "I'm sure you have something to tell me about Dillian, so let me have it."

"You know I went out to the club the other night, right?" Not waiting for a response, Kendra continued, "Well, I ran into Dillian. Actually, he ran into me. Girl, long story short, I think he really has a problem." Glad she got everything about Dillian off of her chest, Kendra let out a breath.

"You saw him? What are you talking about, 'a problem'?" Gracie asked with her eyes squinted and rocking her head from side to side.

"Well, dude was so out of it, not himself at all. If I didn't know him, I would have thought he was on drugs or something. He was going off about you and him breaking up. Yelling, slurring his words. It was a spectacle, girl."

Standing, walking around to the back of the sofa,

Gracie got angry. "If he's drinking and talking about us breaking up, why did we break up?"

Kendra shrugged, turning to Gracie. "That's what I asked him. Before he could say anything, some dudes I ain't ever met before came and got him and took him back to their spot in the club."

Gracie knew that Dillian wasn't even a heavy drinker. Her anger turned into nervousness. Leaning on the sofa, Gracie tried harder to figure Dillian out.

"Oh my goodness! That is so unlike Dillian. He never gets drunk. Tipsy maybe, but that's a different story." Gracie knew she had to do something, anything to find out the real reason for Dillian's actions. "I'm going to call his sister to see if she knows anything. I'm more worried about *him* now instead of the broken relationship."

"Yeah, that's a good idea."

At the club that night, Dillian had repeatedly apologized to Kendra as well, but Kendra dared not to start a whole new conversation that would take them down a different road. Kendra just hoped that her friend found solace in Dillian leaving and prayed that Dillian's apologies weren't as deep as she thought they were. Some things were best left unsaid. At least for the time being.

Gracie's mind traveled at lightning speed as she started questioning Kendra all over again.

"Who did you go out with? Sean?" Gracie asked about Kendra's live-in boyfriend as she sat Indian style on her sofa.

"Where? The club? Oh, uh uh. Me and Tara hit the spot." Knowing that Gracie wasn't the one to pry deep into her personal life, she threw Tara's name in the place of T's, not wanting her best friend to question her going out with other men.

"What did Tara have to say about all of it?"

One lie turned into another. "Nothing. You know Tara; she don't get in the middle of anything." And that was that.

That Saturday afternoon, the ladies sat around talking and watching DVDs back to back until the day had turned to night. Gracie announced that she was getting tired and was going to turn in for the night, and Kendra gathered her things to leave.

"I know you're tired, girl. You about to go home and spend time with Sean?"

"Girl no, I'm about to go home and change and see what's going on at Brooklyns. You want to hang some more?"

"Honey, pah-lease. I already have a hard enough time getting up for eleven o'clock service as it is," Gracie announced as she walked from the hall bathroom, tying her silk head scarf around her braids. "You need to be meeting me up in the place in the morning."

"Yeah. I'll think about it," Kendra said as she gathered her belongings and walked to the door.

"Please do. Be careful and I love ya Ken."

"Love ya too." The best friends hugged.

CHAPTER EIGHT

She started again. It was one thing for Gracie to cross-examine her about Dillian at the club: wanting to know who she was with. But asking about her spending time with her own man and then diving into the church issue, Kendra had just about had it with Gracie. It wasn't like she wasn't grateful and still thankful for all the love that her friend had for her, but her business was her business.

Lauryn Hill was the artist of choice. The soulful, truthful sounds of Lauryn were healing to Kendra as she drove through Dallas headed home to head back out once more. *How did I get here?* It was all Kendra could think as she drove in the direction of the apartment she shared with her current beau, Sean. Kendra drove and immersed herself in her thoughts.

Within the last six months, her world had turned upside down. On top of that, she had had a wreck that could have ended it all. Still not knowing if her survival was for the best, Kendra was struggling with her future. For one, she didn't know how long she could

take Gracie and her motherly approach to their friendship. Gracie had no idea who Kendra really was. Gracie knew her, but she never tried to *know* her.

They met one day in August, approximately one
week before classes actually started on the college
campus. Sitting on her college-sized twin bed, Kendra
sat and read the latest *Essence* magazine, throwing
herself into the cover articles.

Having already unpacked before noon, even before
others had made it on the school grounds, Kendra sat
with her rolled blue jean shorts and baby doll shirt
clinging to her well-developed body. With the dorm
room's door propped open, Gracie walked in with her
parents.

"Hey," Gracie spoke as if she had already been ac-
quainted with Kendra. "I'm Gracie and these are my
parents, Mr. and Mrs. Gregory."

"Hi. It's nice to meet you all," Kendra responded as
she placed the magazine face-down on her bed and
gave them her undivided attention. Offering her hand,
Kendra rose to her feet. "I can leave and give you all
time to unpack if you'd like."

"Nonsense, honey. You two need to mingle and get to
know each other," Mrs. Gregory insisted. When Kendra
saw all the new towels, sheets, and clothes in Gracie's
luggage, Kendra wished she had followed her first mind
and left the room.

Watching Gracie's parents escort her on her freshman
journey, Kendra already assumed that Gracie had it
easy, unlike herself. It took everything in Kendra to push
herself and pack what little clothing she had from her
mother's home and hop on the DART bus. With her
two suitcases trailing close, Kendra made it downtown
to the Greyhound station and rode in silence as the
bus guided her to the college on the outskirts of Dallas.

Having been raised on other people's problems, Kendra was already mentally twenty-five when she was physically eighteen. Surviving on her father's social security, Kendra had to be her own daddy and teach herself what her mother wouldn't.

Herlene tried, but not her best, to continue and raise Kendra in beautiful and booming south Dallas in the eighties after Kendra's father died. But when the streets called her, she answered. Even before Kendra graduated from T.W. Brown Elementary School, she knew for herself that her struggles were going to be more than the other kids' struggles.

No one was looking out for her best interests. Herlene's clubbing habits left young Kendra at home many nights out of the week with a dinner of no more than noodles and crackers. If it hadn't been for the free lunch program at school, Kendra's diet wouldn't have included any protein or vegetables.

As things went from bad to worse, Kendra's uncle came to her rescue. She thought she would find refuge with her mother's younger brother when he showed interest in her welfare. Kendra packed and moved in with him in his efficiency apartment on the east side of Dallas. Just as soon as he gave her dreams, he took them away.

All of her hopes and dreams dissipated the day he started in on her. It started with his brushing the back of his hands on her behind, then the groping. By the time Kendra hit the eighth grade, within two years of living with him, he was commenting on her body and lying on top of her at night and having his way with her. By that time, her innocence, along with her hope, had vanished.

When Kendra told her mother about her uncle's abuse, Herlene apologized profusely and cleaned her-

self up to be the mother that Kendra needed even
though Kendra considered it too late. Kendra's mind
was set on getting all the education she needed in
order to never have to look back. And she did. The day
she met Gracie, her life took on a whole new meaning.

She thought that an education and being away from
her family would make her a different person. She didn't
think she would need counseling, and so the deep secrets of her youth crowded her young adult life. She
was a promiscuous young girl with no one there to
catch her fall.

They were friends and would have to be to remain
business partners, but Kendra was tired of pretending. Keeping up the charade of the two still being best
friends was old. It was hard for Kendra to be overly involved in Gracie's life. Not once had Gracie given her a
friendly shoulder. Gracie had no clue about the physical abuse that Kendra went through as a child.

Gracie had no clue that Kendra loved Sean, but
knew she couldn't be with him. She didn't know that
all the guys Kendra now spent her time with took her
mind off of her true problems. There was too much
that Gracie didn't know.

In her parking space outside of her downtown apartment complex, Kendra turned on her favorite FM station and listened to the loud, jumping, and bopping
music. She suppressed her thoughts and feelings. She
knew that going out always took her mind off of her
problems. Gracie, Sean, and even her secrets would
have to wait.

CHAPTER NINE

Gracie's heart was split in three. On one side she found herself worrying about Dillian. Then, she thought about Kendra's excessive socializing. On the other side, she couldn't help but to think about Marcus, her heart's crush. She knew that, in life, people tend to take the path that leads to what they couldn't have. Gracie wanted Marcus, or at least she wanted to meet Marcus all over again. Prayerfully she decided to be patient. After all, Marcus's girlfriend could have easily chosen any other fitness gym in the big city, but she chose hers. Intervention was at hand.

At work, Gracie half-listened to a message on her home voicemail. She jotted down the 1-888 number that said something about Texas Health. She figured it was OSHA calling to set up a health inspection for the fitness center. Why they hadn't called her office number puzzled her, but she would have to discuss it with them later. The knock on her office door got her attention.

Gracie sat behind her desk and greeted Michelle.

"Hey, Gracie," Michelle said. "I'm so happy that I caught you before I left. Do you have a minute?"

"Uh, sure. What can I do for you?"

"I just wanted my boyfriend to see how your hair was braided. I really like it and when he asked me what I wanted for Christmas, I suggested a new hairstyle."

"Oh!" *Boyfriend*, Gracie thought.

"Do you mind letting him see? Please."

Gracie was caught off guard. For a split second, she couldn't form her words, but she knew that the opportunity was one she couldn't pass up. The time had come and she had to make the best of it.

"Of course," Gracie replied, trying hard to hide her excitement. "Let me grab my keys, and I'll be right behind you."

Butterflies fluttered in Gracie's stomach as she caught up with Michelle in the hallway. Would Marcus be glad to see her? Gracie turned the corner and saw Marcus before he noticed her. Kendra was by his side, which was no surprise at all to Gracie. She figured that the receptionist had told Kendra who Marcus was.

Kendra clasped her hand and smiled. "Oh, looky here," she sung. "Here they come now!"

Gracie held in a laugh at Kendra's *"go get 'em girl"* look as she went in the opposite direction. Turning to Marcus who was grinning from ear to ear, Gracie stood patiently. Before giving her full attention, Gracie looked once more in Kendra's direction. Seeing a beefed-up fellow waiting for her friend, Gracie watched as the two locked lips and disappeared down the hall to their office.

Missing the hints between the two friends, Michelle went forward with her introductions. "Gracie, this is Marcus Jeffries, and Marcus, honey, this is . . ."

"Gracie Elizabeth Gregory!" Marcus finished Michelle's introduction. His intuition was correct. His lost heart had indeed owned the fitness center. No one ever told him, but he played "what if" games in his mind all the time. All of them had to do with Gracie.

Often Marcus had wanted to go inside and find out who the owner was. But because of Michelle's semi-hidden self-esteem problem, he knew that she didn't want him to be around other beautiful women.

"Marcus Bernard Jeffries," Gracie said as she placed her hands on her hips. "Now, how do you like that?" She remembered how he hated his middle name and used it as a weapon.

"Don't be throwing my whole name around in front of strangers."

Michelle arched her eyebrows higher than her Botox allowed.

Gracie breathed easier knowing that Marcus was as happy to see her as she was to see him. From the hug he gave her, she also knew that Michelle regretted wanting the same hairstyle.

Pointing back and forth from Marcus to Gracie, Michelle stood with a stale look on her face. "Oh. The two of you know each other?"

"Yeah," Marcus replied, keeping his smile. "We go way back to those Paris, Texas days. Ain't that right, Gracie?"

The smile on Marcus's face told Michelle all she needed to know. Not wanting to look like a party pooper, she eased the conversation back to the reason for their re-acquaintance.

"Well, anyway, you see her hair? I think it would look nice on me . . . you think?"

"Yeah, it really is nice. I'm not that fond of braided hair, but it really looks nice on you, Gracie." He switched the conversation back to Gracie once more.

Michelle felt a burning ache in her stomach as she watched Marcus talk so friendly to Gracie.

"Thanks," Gracie said, oblivious to Michelle and her anger. "It's my first time having them, but I think they are a great asset when you're on the run a lot."

Marcus nodded in agreement and stepped closer, leaving Michelle behind him. "So, this is you, huh?" He asked, spreading his hands out around the foyer. "How's it been going?"

"Yep, it's all me. Actually, things couldn't be better and how's . . ."

Michelle cleared her throat. Feeling the tension, Marcus cut the conversation short and retrieved his wallet from his warm-up suit. He gave Gracie a card. Gracie shivered inside from the look in Marcus's eyes, a look that begged her to call him.

"Hey," Marcus said "why don't you give me a call so we can do lunch? Catch up on old times? Plus, I can let you in on my boring life," he said with a wink.

"Sounds like a winner, will do." Not realizing what she was doing, Gracie held her breath so that she wouldn't scream.

The two hugged and Marcus was forced to run and catch up with a quick-walking Michelle.

On her way back to their hidden office, down the long hall, Gracie noticed the guy with whom Kendra had disappeared with. A gauche feeling circled the space between them as they said their hellos, passing each other going in the opposite direction.

Walking away from the small refrigerator with a bottle of Gatorade in hand, Kendra was hot on Gracie's heels as soon as her friend made way into their second home. Picking for information, Kendra couldn't wait any longer, but Gracie made her wait.

Gracie looked at Kendra's desk and disheveled clothes. She had a mind to take their gossip in another direction, but thought better of it. Her friend was an adult, and how she spent her time and who she spent it with really wasn't her business.

"So, so, so . . . tell me, girlfriend? How does it feel to have a wish come true right before your eyes? Girl, how you pull that off? Stuff just don't happen that good to me!"

Gracie flopped down on her crowded desk and pressed out a smile. She was still in awe at seeing Marcus. She threw her hands in the air for a bit before finding what to say. "Girl, I can't believe how smooth I acted! Ah!" she laughed.

"Yes indeed, you should get an Oscar for that. So, are you going to call him?"

"Of course I am, but I need to pray that I don't get in over my head. I mean, the guy does have a girlfriend, if you haven't forgotten."

"Who can forget Miss Wanna-be-Johnnie-Cochran?"

Laughing off Kendra's comment, Gracie sat at her desk with Marcus's card still in her hand. She didn't even notice that Kendra had turned and walked out of the office. Gracie sat with her mind on overflow from actually being reacquainted with her old flame.

There was no way she could replace Dillian with

Marcus even if Marcus did become interested. All that she knew was that before the next hurdle, she would most definitely have to complete the first race. She wouldn't mind having Marcus back as a friend at all.

Gracie didn't know what to expect or what not to expect, but she knew that if nothing more, she would let their chance meeting flow. And that is exactly what she planned to do . . . go with the flow.

CHAPTER TEN

On the ride home, Michelle was furious but didn't want to show her true feelings. Right when she thought she had found the perfect man to call her own, she had unintentionally re-introduced him to his long-lost love.

Michelle interrogated Marcus as soon as he entered the car, and she could tell by his facial expression that he was thrilled to have been reunited with Gracie. When she asked Marcus about his relationship with Gracie, he stumbled on words but let her know that they had dated in high school.

"Really?" Michelle responded, sarcasm dripping off each letter. "I should have known by your ever loving expression. Did you forget that I was even standing there, Marcus?"

"Aw Michelle, what is that supposed to mean? Gracie and I were friends before and after we dated. I was just happy to see her, that's all."

Marcus and Michelle had been dating for three months and all was well. Except for a little petty jealousy around other women, he had no significant doubts about her. But his suspicions were growing. Yet and still, with seeing Gracie, he would indeed open his options and not jump in too deep with Michelle, or anyone else for that matter. All in all, he had to do what he had to do. He knew where his heart was and always had been.

"So are you going to start going to the gym there?" Michelle was ready to stop any tricks Marcus had up his sleeves. "Since, you know, your friend owns the place."

After his slight laughter subsided, Marcus knew he had to talk to Michelle. "Look, Michelle. You do not have anything major to worry about. I mean, we are dating and it was agreed that we should date other people as well, right?"

"Yes."

"Well, let's not worry about any of that. Let's just enjoy the time that we have together. I don't know anything about Gracie as she is now and I again am just simply happy to see her again. I will be totally honest with you when I tell you that I probably will visit the gym on a customer level because I patronize African-American businesses and because she's my friend, and I think it's necessary."

"By all means, don't get too offended. I'm a big girl, Marcus; I was just curious. She's your friend and you should support her. She just might need it."

"She might need it? Looks as the though the gym is doing pretty good to me. I mean, the door was swinging while we were there. And that was what? Ten, fifteen minutes at the most?"

"Well, maybe it's a rumor, but word around the gym was that she was dumped not too long ago, and she didn't even see it coming. I heard through the grapevine that she's really down in the dumps. She might need some cheering up."

"Oh. Hmm. Well if that *is* true, so be it. Things happen in life. Good and bad. Isn't that what you told me what happened between you and your last boyfriend?"

Michelle looked Marcus with an *I know he didn't go there* stare. She replied, "Yeah. True, I didn't see my own breakup coming as well . . . but what I heard about Gracie really makes you feel sorry for the girl."

Michelle knew it wasn't fair, but if she were about to lose a promising man, it wouldn't be over someone who could do him more harm than good.

CHAPTER ELEVEN

"What you mean you going out with Shaneka n'em? This yo' third time going out in this one week, ma! What is the deal, yo?"

"Sean, you are tripping! I'm just hanging out. You act like that's all I do," Kendra replied.

"Kendra, for real though. I just got home from work. You ain't spent no time with ya boy and you going out? I tell you what. Let me get cleaned up and I'll step out with you. Okay?"

"Why are you acting, Sean!" Kendra stopped in the middle of their bedroom's floor. She had one Jimmy Choo in her hand and the other on her foot. Kendra didn't like the idea of Sean wanting to tag along and started making excuses. "Dang, it's not about men tonight. It's just me and the girls." Or at least that would be the excuse for tonight. Kendra had plans with T. Not that she liked or even cared about him. T was there just to get her mind off of her situation.

"Oh, so that mean that Gracie going, huh?"

"What?"

"Ya heard me. That mean Gracie going with you then? Or is it just them free-styling females that don't have no attachments and do what they want, huh?" Kicking off his shoes and pulling the bottom of his oxford shirt out of his dress pants. "You know what? Go on and go with your girls, but we need to kiss, hug, snuggle, make love or sump'in before you go. That's your whole purpose and you know it," Sean over-estimated his appeal. "Seem like you don't want to be in the same room with me lately. You cheating?" he asked as he closed in the gap.

Kendra didn't know what to do, but she knew she had to do something and fast. Sean was right. She hadn't been as close to him as normal, but it wasn't because she didn't want to. Being with Sean was the only thing in the world she knew she *really* wanted to do, but knew it wouldn't last long once she came clean.

Cheating hadn't ever been her intention, but it happened. Sean was all that she had ever needed in a man. He was the total package, even down to the drifty dreadlocks. When she had run into him—literally—on a jogging trail almost three years earlier, Sean had been on a business trip. He had taken that same trail she had that lead to the downtown park from her upscale apartment on Bryan. From that day on, on his every visit from the east coast, Sean would make a day available for Kendra and they would spend as much time together as possible. One thing turned into another and Sean changed his lifestyle and moved permanently by Kendra's side in Dallas, Texas.

Their relationship had taken them up a notch. Talk about marriage swarmed between the two, children, and house shopping. All things halted surely for Kendra, just hours before she had the car accident.

The news she received put everything in a total different perspective. Marriage to Sean, work, and even living weren't on her list any longer. Kendra liked to think she was protecting Sean. She allowed their relationship to lose the grip that was once solid.

Smacking her lips as she leaned over and put her shoe on, Kendra ignored both of his requests. "Look, I'll be home later. We can talk then, but I'm not about to get undressed and do all of this over," she said, pointing to her face, fully made up with Bobbi Brown's collection.

As she came to the same height as Sean, he grabbed her and kissed her with all of his might. "Kendra, I love you. I wouldn't have ever come to Texas if it weren't for you, ma. Don't do me dirty. When you come home we need to talk," he said as he released his girlfriend, whom he badly wanted to be his wife. It was all on her.

She knew Sean had an inkling that she was backing away from the idea of marriage because she hadn't moaned a word about a church, dress, or anything that related to the special day that most women long for. Since the car wreck, he had wondered if she had a change of heart. No, was her response because it was the truth. She was holding out as long as possible.

She knew that when Sean said they needed to talk, he really meant talk. Kendra grabbed her Chloe bag and headed toward the front door on her mission to drink as much as possible. For the sole purpose of having to sleep with Sean when she got home, Kendra knew she would have to be intoxicated in order to give herself to someone she didn't even deserve. She just hoped he wouldn't question her when she brought up wearing protection first.

CHAPTER TWELVE

A couple of weeks after seeing Marcus again, Gracie had been on a natural high. But when reality hit her again, so did her nightmares.

Since she still had the same nightmares about Dillian, Gracie was determined not to miss church service the following Sunday to hear the Word. She prayed that it was a message directly for her and longed for complete peace from whatever it was that was crowding her nights.

She woke up before her alarm went off. She showered and dressed warmly in a corduroy skirt suit to go to eight o'clock Sunday morning service. Her church on the north side of Dallas was having their Thanksgiving program that Sunday instead of later in the week and she didn't want to miss it.

Unlike her hometown church, which had a traditional prayer line, the church that she adopted requested the congregation to write down their prayer requests and put them in the appropriate prayer box. Although she had nothing against this method, Gracie could have used some foot stomping, hand clapping praise and hands-on approach to feel God's love. Nevertheless, Gracie placed her prayer request in the box on the outside of the sanctuary door, made her way into service, and went through with the service worshipping the heavens above.

"With my hands lifted up ... and my mouth filled with praise ... with a heart of thanksgiving ... I will bless thee oh Lord ..."

Gracie joined in with the praise team that faced the congregation. She worshipped the Lord and didn't ask for anything in particular. She knew that God knew her heart and that her heart was still heavy with Dillian and his disappearance. Quietly, she called out to her Heavenly Father.

"I don't know what it is, God, but if you will just fight my battle. I can't figure it out, but the Word says that you will wipe away all the tears from my eyes. Lord please take the pain away."

By the time the Word came forth and the pastor spoke from John 8:12, "He that followeth me shall not walk in darkness," Gracie knew that the sermon was meant for her. Writing her notes and making sidebars for later reading, Gracie knew that God would bring her out if she would just follow Him.

After church service, Gracie returned home to get her luggage. She was heading out to her parents' for the first winter holiday. However, her mind went from luggage to Marcus. She decided to call him to see if he wanted to meet for coffee before she left.

Being reacquainted over the last few months had been more on a professional level with the two meeting and talking to each other at the gym. Thinking it would be a nice change of scenery, Gracie called.

"Hello?" He answered after the first couple of rings.

"Hey, Marcus, how are you?"

"What's up, Gracie? I'm good and you?" She heard a smile in his voice.

"Oh, just about to head down I-30, going home. I was calling to see if you wanted to meet for coffee before I headed that way. I have to pass your way to get there anyway." Marcus lived in Rockwall, which was indeed on the way.

"That sounds like a great idea, but actually I'm trying to tie up everything before I head out myself. Why don't we just get in touch when I get there and do something? I'm sure your parents wouldn't mind me stealing you for a few hours."

Gracie knew they wouldn't care if he kept her forever. "I'm sure they wouldn't either. But uh, isn't Michelle going to be there with you?" She held her breath and waited on the answer.

"Uh, no. Why would she go to Paris with me?"

"Well, I just figured that's what couples did for the holidays. Sorry."

"Don't be sorry. That *is* what couples do, but Michelle and I are not a couple. We are dating."

"Oh."

"Look, I'm pretty sure I know where you got your information from, and I won't be mad at your parents. Why don't I just explain it to you over dinner tonight in P-town."

"I'd love to."

When Gracie hung up the phone, she was raring to head out of town, especially knowing that she would get to see Marcus at home. Besides that, she was mentally ready for a break. Her mind was already exhausted just thinking of all the work would await her return. More meetings, more quotes, more aerobic classes to teach. She wanted to finalize a location for her second fitness center.

So the little prissy had been lying all the time. She hoped that she would remember to call Kendra and give her the latest gossip.

Right as she was about to get up and head to the door, Gracie's phone rang. The name Rebecca McNab registered on the caller ID. Gracie knew to sit and take the call, ceasing other thoughts. Gracie had left a message a while back, but Rebecca hadn't returned the call. Gracie knew that she needed to talk to Dillian's sister right then and there.

"Hello?" Gracie answered.

"Gracie?"

"Yes? Hey, Rebecca. How are you?" Hand to her chest, Gracie slowly sat down.

"I'm okay, Gracie, but of course not the best. But the question is: how are you? I'm sorry I'm just now getting back with you." Rebecca's concern let Gracie know she already knew what had happened between her and Dillian.

Gracie shook her head "yes" as if Rebecca could see her, "I'm doing better. I'm trying to make it. Is Dillian there with you?"

"No, he's not. Gracie, he didn't only leave you, he left the whole family. No one has talked to him. Actually, we don't even know if he's still alive."

"What?!"

Gracie found out that whatever it was that Dillian was running from didn't only concern the two of them. Though it eased her pain a little, it also brought more turmoil in her mind. All she could think about was the "problem" that Dillian had and how he obviously felt he couldn't talk to anyone close to him.

"What is he running from?" was all Gracie could repeatedly ask herself. He hadn't left anything that hinted at his problem or problems. From his sister, Gracie found out that he ditched his two-way and cell phone, hadn't been training at the gym, and couldn't be found through a phone or an apartment in his name anywhere in the city.

"What could he be running from, Gracie? Do you have a clue?"

"Rebecca, even though I'm embarrassed to admit it, I haven't a clue. I feel so stupid having lived with someone and not knowing that they were going through something so severe. I didn't see it. Maybe it was me. Maybe it was just me."

"Gracie, you can't blame yourself, that's for sure. Whatever Dillian is going through, it's personal. Let's pray that he's doing the right thing."

"My prayers have already started."

Once in Paris, Gracie spent a couple of hours with her parents. Then, the phone rang, and Mr. Gregory answered it.

"Hey there, Mr. Gregory, how are you?" Marcus said.

"Aw, I can't complain about anything. And yourself?"

"I guess I'll be doing fine once you let me know your daughter has arrived."

"Oh, yeah? Well, that girl that calls herself my daughter and already eating up my food? Yeah, she has arrived, alright." Pausing for laughter, Mr. Gregory ushered Gracie to the telephone. "Hold on while I give her the phone, Marcus."

Talking with Mr. Gregory had always been a treat for Marcus. He adored both of Gracie's parents and made sure he dropped by to check on them whenever he was in town. He enjoyed their company as much as they did his.

Before handing the phone over to Gracie, Mr. Gregory told Marcus that he was happy that the two of them had finally crossed paths once again. Marcus couldn't help but smile inside. Gracie had always meant a great deal to him. The love he had for her had surpassed any love he'd ever had for any of his other girlfriends. By the looks of things with his current dating habits, Gracie would never be matched.

Gracie knew everything about him; from his boyhood pranks and young man mistakes, but she had never given up on him. She just accepted that he wasn't ready for a commitment bigger than what they already had. If it wasn't for his desire to test the waters, Marcus knew they would have been married already. He also knew that he did the right thing by leaving off on a good note. That alone had promised him a happy return, which is what he knew this was.

"Hey, you made it?" Gracie asked when she came to the phone. Marcus could tell that she was excited to hear from him.

"About thirty minutes ago. Are you busy?"

"Boy, did you even get to kiss your momma hello before you called me?" She laughed. "Of course I'm busy. My momma got me making the grocery list. Nothing major though. What's up?" Gracie winked her eye at her mother. Mrs. Gregory was about to go off on her for saying her chores were "nothing major." Gracie put her index finger over her mouth, calming her mother down.

"Okay, well why don't you go ahead and finish up with your folks. And if it's okay with you, I'll come by and pick you up about, let's say, eight?"

"That's fine. I'll be ready."

And ready she was. After hurrying her mother in

the supermarket, Gracie raced into the house to get
ready for her date.

She felt guilty about the date, but she knew she had
to move on with her life. Gracie knew she still had to
add Dillian to her agenda when she returned home.
Beyond anything, she had to make sure, for herself,
that all was well with him. Before heading into the
shower, Gracie knelt down and said a silent prayer.
She asked God to be with Dillian, give strength where
needed, comfort him, and let all be well.

Gracie was surprised when she took in its romantic
setting at the restaurant. She eyed Marcus and wondered what his plans were, not just for that night, but
also for the rest of his life. She shook her head and
smiled to herself. *I will not rush anything.*

"Oh, this is nice," she said. "My parents told me
about this place."

It was a little out of the way, but Marcus was feeling
romantic and wanted the ambiance to be just right.
Besides, Marcus hoped that one day Gracie would be
his, and this could be the perfect spot to get things
started.

"Yeah, it's a pretty nice place," he conceded. He
smiled down into Gracie's face and slid her chair out.
"Have a seat."

After their waitress came over and they placed their
orders, there was a slight pause between the two.

"You look nice, Gracie," Marcus said, filling the
pause with an earnest compliment.

Gracie giggled and blushed. "You sound like you just
met me."

"Well, I did, and I hope to get to know a little more
about the *new* you."

"Okay, I'm game. But aren't you supposed to be clearing something up?"

Marcus thought quietly for a second before he remembered. "You're right! About Michelle, right?"

"Right."

"Well, we are definitely not *together*. I'm sorry if she's been saying that and I plan on talking to her about it, but that's not the case. We're just dating. Remember the kids down here I was telling you about over the phone? The ones that I, along with other coaches, have been scouting? Well, when I needed a lawyer to handle paperwork or what have you, she was that lawyer. That turned into dating." Marcus continued, "She's a nice girl, but her self-esteem is one thing I can't deal with . . . I mean, I'm constantly letting her know that she worries about the wrong things."

"Really? I'm sorry to hear that. Well, I can tell that Michelle likes you from how she talks about you at the gym, so I just want to let you know that I'm not trying to come in between anything you two have going on. I'm merely catching up with an old friend."

With his eyebrow raised in disbelief, Marcus also raised his glass of wine for a toast. "To friends."

Conversation flowed so seamlessly between the pair that it was hard to believe they ever had a break in their friendship. As each topic of conversation ended, another one began. Neither one wanted the night to end.

Things came to a halt when Marcus asked about Dillian and why he up and left Gracie. Her face went rigid and her mind blank. She was three seconds away from fainting and falling from her chair.

"I'm sorry," Marcus said quickly. "Was I out of line?"

Taking a sip of water, Gracie was at a loss for words.

"Uh. Well, no you're not out of line," she whispered. "It's just that I try not to think about it much." She was still embarrassed about the whole thing. Discussing a walk out by a boyfriend with an old boyfriend was at the top of the list for embarrassments.

"Well, we most definitely don't have to talk about it."

"Thanks, I appreciate it."

Despite the awkward moment, they were able to move back into normal conversation. They talked about their plans for the future and what was going on with their lives.

Gracie took in Marcus's excitement over his new position as head coach with a university in the Dallas metropolitan area, which allowed him to move from Houston and closer to home. He was proud of being the first black man to take on the position, but even more exciting to him . . . and equally so to Gracie, was that Marcus had no plans of leaving Dallas anytime soon. Gracie could tell he was hoping that that was a plus for her. It was.

The two smiled at each other across the table.

"Do you remember when I said that if neither of us were married by twenty-five, we should get married?" Marcus asked.

With eyes wide and a half grin on her face, Gracie couldn't believe that Marcus had remembered something that was so meaningful to her. "Of course I remember. Why, you want to get married?" She joked as she picked up her glass of wine and brought it to her mouth.

"I might." Noticing the pale look on Gracie's face, Marcus grabbed for her hand. "I'm just kidding. See, that's what you get for being so goofy. Nah, I was just seeing if you remembered."

"Ha!" Gracie laughed, but her heart was beating like a jackhammer. "You are so funny." She playfully slapped at his hand.

As the laughter subsided, Marcus said, "Seriously though, I thought about you a lot when we were apart. It was hard getting over you, but I did it. The bad thing is that I only did it because I had to. I mean, I wanted to do right by you and I know I was leaning the wrong way while we were together."

Marcus cleared his throat and took in the raised eyebrow and slight smirk that presented itself on Gracie's face.

"I know, I know," he continued. "I did a lot of stupid stuff and I regret it all. I was young and dumb, but if you let me make it up to you, I'm going to do just that."

Her eyes glazed, Gracie felt as if she were dreaming the words out of Marcus's mouth. But she knew that it was all real. Her reaction said neither "yes" nor "no," but "maybe." Gracie's heart was in her mouth and she chose to respond only with a smile.

CHAPTER THIRTEEN

A whirlwind. That's what Gracie felt was happening to her. The feeling alone had her daydreaming. Her desires intertwined into a make-believe world, except she knew it was all so real. Being able to spend personal time with Marcus was overwhelming, but very appealing to her heart. Marcus's smile had made her time away from Dillian easier and lighter.

Back in Dallas, Gracie took over a class for one of her contract trainers. She knew it would benefit Laila and help her with the extra pounds she'd put on over Thanksgiving. Gracie arose even earlier than normal and opened the gym for the day. Faces that she didn't usually have the pleasure of seeing and people that she wouldn't have the chance to meet otherwise, was a given with the class at four in the morning.

One of the first people in the class happened to be Tara, whom she'd met through Kendra. The last time they had come face to face was at the hospital the night that Kendra had her near-fatal accident. Tara was actually the one to call Gracie to tell her about the situation.

That night, Tara met Gracie at the hospital's entrance and led her up the elevator to the floor Kendra was on. After they made enough small talk to settle their nerves, Gracie asked where Kendra had been and what had happened.

"I don't know exactly where she was but she had called me just before it happened . . . crying hysterically! I thought something had happened then, but—"

"So she had the accident *after* the phone call or before?"

"Yep. After," Tara replied as she looked at Gracie as if she wanted to continue.

"Hmm. I wonder what was going on with her?" Gracie wondered aloud, not specifically waiting for an answer. She looked up and saw Sean. Gracie walked his way right as Tara readied herself to continue their short conversation.

Now the morning class had begun, and Gracie gave a brief smile and wave. She geared up with her microphone and headphones. Gracie knelt and looked through a group of compact discs, finding one suitable for the class. Gracie was satisfied when she ran across a good ole Vickie Winans hit.

After class, Gracie replenished her energy with a full bottle of water. She lingered a little too long and almost forgot that she wanted speak to Tara when she saw the tall, local model leaving the hot and steamy room.

"Tara!" Gracie yelled across the emptying room, her dry throat slightly choking on the remainder of the water. Tara turned and gave Gracie a friendly wave and turned once more on her way.

"Tara . . . wait!" Gracie jumped down from her space and headed for the door. "Girl, what you trying to make me do? Are you paying me back for the workout?"

"Funny! Girl, no. I'm sorry. I didn't know you wanted to chat. How've you been, Gracie?"

"Girl," Gracie moved further from the door, allowing one of the last pupils out of the classroom, "I'm doing. Look, I don't know if you know about me and Dillian, but. . . ."

"Yeah, I'm sorry about that."

"Thanks. But I just wanted to apologize on his behalf. Kendra told me that you all saw him at the club a while back and how he was acting. That is too embarrassing," Gracie continued as she faced toward the floor.

"Huh? *We* saw him where?" Tara asked as she retied her sweatshirt around her waist and crossed her long, lanky arms.

"At the club," Gracie stared in confusion. "I don't know which one, but Kendra had said—

"Gracie, I haven't gone out to a club since *last* summer. Girl, Kendra is tripping. Listen . . ." Tara looked around before she continued. "Can we go into your office?"

Confused by Tara's words, Gracie agreed. Right as they turned down the hall, Tara started on their conversation, ceasing their walk and continuing their talk.

"I've wanted to mention this to you, but since I don't see you often, I didn't know how I was going to talk to you. I guess all things happen for a reason, huh?"

"Well I wasn't with Kendra that night," Tara continued, "but I know about it. I don't know what Dillian's problem is and you know I'm not one to get into people's business, but, anyway, Kendra was out with some dude that night, but I don't know who exactly."

Gracie described T for Tara. "I wonder if it's the dude we ran into at the mall a while back. Do you know him? A young-looking dude? All that I got from his name was T."

"With T?" Tara asked with disgust, trying not to let Gracie in on her secret pain. "You know what, it wouldn't amaze me. Yep, that's T alright. I'm sure he's become one of Kendra's new 'men friends.' I don't know what has gotten into her, but since she's been changing, I don't really spend that much time with her."

"So she *is* cheating on Sean then, huh? What is going on with that girl? I see men coming through here. She says that she's training them."

"Oh, she's training them all right. But not like you would. You know what I mean. I'm praying for Kendra, and she is still my girl, well, *was*, but that's teenage what she's doing. We are in the real world and I'm not with it."

"Right." Gracie quietly agreed with her head down.

"Well, I better get going. I have a photo shoot this morning with Saj Studios. But please don't tell Kendra I told you about me not being in the club with her. I think she really is going through something." Tara wanted to elaborate more on Kendra and T, but decided against it. Just because she was going to end her friendship with Kendra, she didn't feel as though she should try to persuade Gracie to do the same.

"Don't worry, I won't." Thinking fast, Gracie remembered what she was going to ask as Tara started walking back down the hall. "Tara. Remember when Kendra had the wreck and you said that she was crying on the line *before* the accident . . . do you know what she was crying about?"

Rewinding her memory to Kendra's car wreck, Tara closed her eyes.

"You know. I don't quite know. She never really spilled anything out of the crying. All she said was that she needed someone to talk to and that she couldn't talk to you because you'd start throwing God all up in the midst."

Shocked by the comment, Gracie threw her head back in disbelief, wanting Tara to continue. "Really?"

"Yeah. She just kept saying her life was over, her life was over. I asked her a few days later at the hospital what was going on, but that's when she stopped talking. Said it was nothing." Tara shrugged her shoulders and checked her workout watch, making sure she wasn't running late.

"She never told me anything," Gracie said, looking down at her shoestring that lay on either side of her shoe. "Shoot, I never knew Kendra went through drama at any point."

Eyebrows arched, Tara seemed shocked by Gracie's statement.

"Where have you been, Gracie?"

"Huh?"

Walking back to Gracie, Tara continued.

"Gracie, honestly, I've known Kendra longer than you have and I don't know how you can still stand to be around her. I sometimes let things that she does go simply because of all the drama in her life. I mean . . ."

"Me and Kendra are like sisters . . . We are there for each other."

"I hope you're right about that. But as for me, I know I'm through now."

"What do you mean? 'Now' you know you're through?" Gracie asked with squinted eyes.

"Well, at first it was all in my mind, but when you asked about me being at the club with Kendra, then you asked about the guy and I said I didn't know . . . when you said T. Umm, T is the guy I was talking to, really into, but I felt like something was going on with him and Kendra. Now I know."

"Oh my goodness," Gracie walked even closer to Tara and gave her a hug. "I'm sorry, Tara, I had no idea. Please believe me."

"Gracie, I know what type of person you are. I'm not worried about it. You and Kendra are friends, not twins. Don't even worry about it. I'll get over it." She hugged Gracie just a little longer than an acquaintance would. Tara teared up when she realized that Kendra really had betrayed her. "Look, I better go or I'll be late. Thank you, Gracie, for the talk . . . thanks for the hug."

Gracie released Tara. "You can call me anytime, Tara. I hope you'll still be coming to the gym."

"Girl, and you know it. I'll definitely call you, maybe we can do lunch or something."

"Sounds good." Gracie turned and went into her office. She hadn't decided whether to put Kendra on the spot when she got in or just sweep it under the rug. One thing she knew for sure was that Kendra was becoming someone she didn't know.

Now she knew that Kendra was cheating on Sean. Gracie still wanted to know what secret Kendra was keeping. She was worried and knew that as much as she wanted to be in the loop with Kendra, she knew her friend wouldn't tell her.

"Lord, give me strength to deal with all this. Please keep Kendra out of harm's way and give her strength to deal with whatever it is that she is going through. I need you, Lord, but I think she needs you a little more right now."

CHAPTER FOURTEEN

Dillian had been hiding in the hospital under a false name for the last few weeks. At first, Dillian thought about his career, his status, and his fans and decided that anonymity would be best. Later, as he battled with the cold medical facility, he just didn't care if any one knew him or not. He gave up on life and laid limp as his doctor ranted about his condition.

"Mr. McNab, I'm telling you from a doctor's perspective and someone who sees these cases all the time. If you don't take your medication as prescribed, your visits will become more frequent and more serious . . ."

Between his listening spells, Dillian knew he had to grasp the whole ordeal. He was HIV positive and there was no way to get around it. The only thing he could do was accept it or not. And at the moment, he had no intentions of accepting the diagnosis.

If he accepted it, that would mean taking many pills daily. Half of the names of pills were hard for him to even pronounce. A definite change in his life would come. Again, if he accepted that he was in fact HIV positive, there still wouldn't be a cure. He would only be fighting a war he wasn't sure he would win before the virus took over. In fact, he felt there would be only a slim chance for him to win.

If he continued on the path he was now on—not accepting that he had HIV—he would certainly get worse. Every day that he refused to take his medication meant another day for the virus to invade his body and destroy his CD4+ cells. It meant another day that his body would continue to lose its ability to produce new cells to replace the ones that were being destroyed. This was only *one* of the results Dillian remembered the doctor listing if he didn't accept his condition and deal with it.

He knew that most people would opt to take the medication, but he wasn't like most people. As a well-known body builder, Dillian had won hundreds of awards, including winning Mr. Universe. It was hard for Dillian to remember those accolades and think that all that he had built could be destroyed so easily.

At least once every hour, Dillian's life flashed before his eyes: shocking the fitness world by retiring at age twenty-five, starting up his own training business that earned him top clientele, and coming out of retirement just a year later to compete in the Olympics. He started a rigorous schedule to get his body into competitive shape, but he had help. He started with his steroid shots once again, never thinking that his secret needle would ever infect him; it hadn't in the past . . . but his past was not his present.

It wasn't until this year that Dillian had started to feel ill, or at least his body felt different. It wasn't until he was having sweats, the fevers, and the near-fainting spells that Dillian went to a doctor, and even then it was because of Gracie's suggestion.

Dillian was stunned when the doctor asked if he'd taken an HIV/AIDS test before. HIV was the furthest thing from his mind. Dillian knew who he had been with, and for the last two years, he had only been with Gracie, and they had used protection. However, he got his test results, nearly four months before he left Gracie. The problem was that Dillian had no idea where the infection originated. He got the medication from a close friend, who got it from someone else, who of course, got it from someone else. At the time, Dillian was confident that the underground supply was a clean deal. It was as legit as it could be; but clean it wasn't.

When he pulled his vehicle into the park, he didn't even realize which neighborhood he was in and he didn't care for that matter. *Should have known better* was all he kept saying over and over without any healing for the pain he was feeling.

Sitting deep into the cushion on the driver's side, Dillian peered out the window and watched a family huddle around the swing sets afar off. Without knowing they were present, Dillian wiped away the tears that fled from his eyes. He thought about his own children that he would never get to enjoy at the park.

"How stupid," he mouthed as he thought about the abrupt, as he thought, end to his life. Slamming his hand against the thick plastic on the steering wheel, Dillian no longer fought the tears. With his forehead plastered against the navigation device, Dillian reminisced.

He couldn't help but grimace as he thought back on the many times he'd actually allowed needles to touch his backside, his arms, or his legs. In thinking on one time in particular, wondering if it had been the point in time when his blood had actually been diluted, Dillian became disgusted with his actions.

"Man, where's it at," Dillian hurriedly asked as he'd rushed into the unlocked door to Trey's house. "I got a plane to catch."

"That's right," Trey responded, walking out of the fogged kitchen. Holding his lips tight around the marijuana that was already housed in his lungs, Trey shooed Dillian into one of the back rooms. "You gotta go check in for the Olympics or something like that, huh?"

"Yeah, man. Which way?" Dillian didn't pause for small talk. Making his way into the hallway's restroom, he looked around for the medication. "Ain't no vial in here, man," he hollered.

When Trey stuck his head around the door and into the restroom, he pointed to where Dillian could find his medication. "It's right there." He pointed to the needle that lay on the back of the sticky sink.

"This needle right here?" Dillian pointed without touching the made up concoction. With his eyebrow questioning the air, Dillian's answer came after a misplaced Trey yelled from the next room over.

As he looked down at the needle, it was only half of a second that Dillian second-guessed his decision to continue with his plans. Shrugging his thoughts of wondering who put together the needle, Dillian pulled down his workout pants, picked up the unfamiliar injection device and commenced to ready his aim.

Not knowing or even feeling the trickling of blood that ran from the injection spot, down his skin, Dillian reappeared in what should have been the living area of the house. Seeing five unfamiliar faces squeezed together on one loveseat: one shooting up a substance into his vein and the others smoking from a shared glass pipe, Dillian shook his head in disgust.

Not being able to stand the sight of the addict thrusting the needle so hard and deep into his veins, Dillian walked toward the exit yelling out Trey's name, waiting to see if he would appear. When he didn't see or hear any footsteps coming down the hall, Dillian opened the door and scurried from his friend's property.

Oh my God, what have I done?, Dillian thought as he grabbed the thin hospital covers, pulling them up to his shoulders as he turned to his side, avoiding his doctor all together.

Once diagnosed, Dillian contemplated many ways to cope. He didn't stay around long enough at the doctor's office to get information about the serious virus. He only linked his *new* life with the life he had heard about in the movies he had seen. All he knew was the diagnosis, taking medication that made you sick if you weren't already, and then dying.

He figured he'd just speed up the process and put an end to something that hadn't meant any good for anyone. Dillian played with the idea of suicide on different levels, but none stood.

"Your life doesn't have to end now," was all he remembered the doctor trying to convince him as he sat in disbelief in the cold room. How could he believe that coming from someone who only gave the information and didn't have to take it in for himself? He couldn't shake the idea of his body, the body he had worked so hard on over the years, becoming thin to the bone.

Dillian knew that if he decided to come out with his infection and take his medication, he could lose everything. Honest or not, most people would shun him. Eventually, he would lose everything he had worked so hard for, including Gracie.

The night he found out about his infection, he told Gracie he had to leave on a business trip. Without going home to gather clothes or any personal belongings, Dillian drove as far as he could. He knew he couldn't just run away, but he had to air out his thoughts. He had to decide which way to turn.

If he had only gone to the doctor one month earlier— one month—he would never have surprised Gracie with the engagement ring of her dreams. Just one month earlier, he wouldn't have confessed all of his love to her only to end up breaking her heart. Her heart would be more than broken if somehow, some way she contracted the virus. But in Dillian's memory, there was no possibility . . . or was there?

When he thought of sitting Gracie down and explaining the situation to her, he tried to keep in mind that she was a God-fearing woman and that she would forgive him and stand by his side. Then reality hit him hard. It wasn't like he was bringing home a baby from an affair. The "baby" he carried would never grow older and leave home; it was there to stay.

He wasn't perfect, but he never did anything intentionally to hurt Gracie. He knew that, in her eyes, he was close enough to perfect. To him she *was* perfect. They were friends first, which allowed them to successfully transform their relationship into an honest, trustworthy companionship. He had broken her trust. Now he was too afraid to let her know.

As he lay in the hospital bed, he realized that it wouldn't be long after he was released that he would be coming back. He had no plans on taking medications or making anything "seem" okay. Drinking had become the only way of coping. Drinking *was* his therapy.

He didn't want to believe his new life; however, he

wasn't far enough into denial to continue hurting others. Dillian knew he just wouldn't be able to have sex again. He knew he would never have a serious relationship with a woman because he would always think she was pretending to love him out of pity. He knew he would never have kids to carry on his name. *The faster I can get this over with, the faster everyone can move on.*

As he thought about wasting away, he felt guilty. Guilt ran through his veins as he sat in a hospital room without his family or friends knowing his whereabouts. He'd ditched his pager and cell phone the day he left the apartment. He had his personal assistant call his clients and let them know that he wouldn't be able to make appointments and didn't leave a date when he would return. The road he was traveling down was that of destruction.

On top of all that, the health department hotline had gotten in contact with him to let him know that they had yet to get in touch with Gracie to give her the information that she needed. He had no idea what else could go wrong, but he knew there was more to come. Letting Gracie know was only the beginning.

CHAPTER FIFTEEN

On a cold December afternoon, Marcus and Gracie drove behind Gracie's realtor, who had found a site for her second gym. Marcus pulled up to the site and grabbed Gracie's hand just as she was about to bound out the door like an eager child.

"Can we talk for a second?" he asked.

Gracie noticed his tone and nodded. She raised her index finger to her realtor and mouthed the words *hold up* through the door's window.

"What's up?" Gracie asked.

Not caring if he looked corny, Marcus looked serious while he cleared his throat and focused on Gracie.

"You know Michelle?" he shook his head, regretting the question as soon as it was out his mouth. *Of course she knew Michelle.*

"Uh, yeah." Gracie turned her body toward Marcus and folded her arms across her chest. Her mind was already jumping to conclusions, and she felt her cheeks begin to tingle with heat. "What's going on?"

"Well," Marcus began. "I haven't seen much of her since before Thanksgiving."

Gracie sighed and relaxed, but she continued to listen intently.

"Okay," she said, allowing Marcus to go on.

"I have really been enjoying what we are doing, Gracie. I mean, the way we have clicked as if time never came between us is really nice. Even though I know there is more that you have to learn about the present me, and vice-versa, I just want to let you know that my feelings for you are making me want to date you exclusively."

Marcus took Gracie's silence as a good sign. "As far as Michelle, she is a nice girl, but she doesn't really move me the way you do. I know this is soon, but I prayed for God to point me in the direction of my wife and well . . ."

"Goodness!" was all Gracie could say. She pressed her back against the door and her hand fluttered up to her mouth. When the word settled, Gracie looked at Marcus and wished she had found a better response.

"Don't take that the wrong way," she said as she took hold of one of Marcus's hands. "Believe me, it was 'goodness' in a good way." She continued, "It's just that my heart has been going back and forth about Dillian. I welcome the idea of us starting to date, but I have to make sure that I've left no stone unturned, you know, until I find out that everything is okay with him."

Smiling, he knew Gracie wanted the same. Yet, he realized she had to do what she had to do. That was just the type of person she was.

"I understand, and I won't step in your way at all."

That remark alone let Gracie know that a bond, something special was forming between the two of them and she knew that she too wanted more.

CHAPTER SIXTEEN

Over the following weeks, things for Marcus and Gracie progressed even more. When Gracie found out that Michelle had switched her class for Kendra's, she knew Marcus was for real. She felt bad about having come between Michelle and Marcus. But Marcus had said that they were not a couple, and she had no reason not to believe him.

Walking through the entrance to Marcus's house, Gracie was exhausted. She had taken the latter part of the day off to meet with Dillian's sister, talking about his whereabouts.

"Thanks for inviting me to dinner. I am too tired to move a muscle," Gracie told him.

"No problem. I figured you had enough on your plate right now between choosing a site and Dillian."

Conversation skills alone put Marcus above the rest. Most men that Gracie had come in contact with were never able to talk about the other men in her life, let alone someone she had planned on marrying. Gracie could see that Marcus was a changed man. Not only in how he talked, but also in how he acted and how he had let God into his life. It made her proud to know that he had given his life over to God and hadn't looked back. If there was one thing a man had to have in order to be her partner for life, it was to have a relationship with The Most High.

"So did you two have any luck?" Marcus asked. "How's your search going?"

"Oh, it's going," Gracie slid her words out in a comical way. "Nowhere that is. I just think I need to leave it alone. If he cared or really wanted me to know—well, us to know—he would have talked with someone."

"Do you think he could have been in trouble or something? Needed money?" Marcus asked with concern in his voice.

"I seriously doubt that. He was just about to purchase a boat! It was one of the reasons we started arguing in the first place. I think." She was no longer sure about that detour in her and Dillian's relationship.

"Oh."

The subject was still rather sour for Gracie, even though she knew she would get through it better if she talked about it. She just needed more time. Even though Marcus had lent his ear and was all too ready to give her a chance to vent, Gracie didn't want to run him away, so she eased the conversation in a different direction.

Later, as the two moved from the dining room into the living area, the silkiness of Marcus's sofa and her comfort around him put her so at ease that Gracie fell asleep in mid-sentence. Half an hour later, she awakened, finding Marcus staring down at her in amusement.

"Oh, you're up now?" he asked, before laughing.

"I'm sorry," she said. She blushed when she realized her head rested in his lap. "You should have pinched me."

"No." He stroked her hair. "You obviously needed the rest."

Marcus lowered his head in an attempt to kiss Gracie's forehead. Without a second thought, she slid up so that their lips met. Although it wasn't the first time they had kissed since their chance meeting, it was the most intimate. The kiss wasn't lustful, but warm and tasteful. It was just right. It made them feel as if the kiss was long overdue.

Their harmless embrace progressed into a passionate longing. However, when their eyes opened at the exact same time, they mutually agreed that their passion needed to be halted before anything further took place.

"I'd better get up and get out of here," Gracie said. She sat up and stretched, trying to get her thoughts together.

"Yeah, it's getting pretty late." Marcus tried to avoid looking at Gracie for fear that she could see how much he wanted her. "You're welcome to take some leftovers for lunch tomorrow if you'd like." Marcus felt the heat from his pants leave. The space where Gracie had laid her head had cooled, triggering him to get up from his seat.

"That'll be great!" Gracie said with way too much enthusiasm.

She picked up her pager that sat beside her purse on the coffee table. There was a message from Kendra.

"Darn it!"

"What is it?" Marcus asked with a raised voice as he plastic-wrapped a lunch plate for Gracie.

"Kendra just text messaged me and said she won't be in tomorrow, again."

"What's wrong with her, yo?"

Sharing a laugh with Marcus as he mocked Kendra's east-coast-wanna-be slang, Gracie answered. "She's been sick with a cold or something for about two weeks. I told her it was nothing but pregnancy, but she threatened me, saying I'm trying to jinx her."

The shared laugh took her mind off of having to get up early to find a substitute for Kendra's class.

As she prepared to leave, Gracie thought back on her evening with Marcus. She couldn't understand how she was happy yet sad, all at the same time. She couldn't get too excited about Marcus, especially as she sought closure with Dillian. It definitely wasn't that she doubted that Marcus could be a good man, she just couldn't move forward with the thought of Dillian turning out *not* to be her "good" man.

Guilt filled her and she made a B line to the door.

"What's wrong? Is there something on your mind?"

"Uh. No, I'm good. I just better get out of here. Call me in the morning, okay?"

"And you know I will. Make sure you call me when you make it in the house." He walked Gracie to her car in the cool of the night. They finished the night with a kiss and parted ways.

CHAPTER SEVENTEEN

On the ride home, Gracie gathered her thoughts about Kendra. She knew it was time to have a conversation with her. Before making the right turn onto the clear highway, Gracie reached in her purse for her phone. Gracie couldn't come up with anything to break the ice before Kendra answered the call.

"Hello?" Kendra answered. She sounded as if she were deep in a hole somewhere.

"Wow. You really do sound bad. So you're not going to be in tomorrow? Do you have an appointment with your doctor?"

"Nah. I'm okay. I have my medication. I think my body is just tired. I just need to rest."

Gracie got off I-30 and took the ramp to Central Expressway. "Humph. You think? I think you've been doing a little too much of everything here lately. I'm surprised it took your body this long to catch up with your running around."

"What are you talking about, Gracie? I have a cold . . . ."

"Yeah, but . . . well. I've been meaning to ask how you've been doing."

"Huh?"

"Come on now, Kendra, you know I'm not that far in denial. You call me a black blonde, but I'm far from it. I know you've been creeping out on Sean. You stay in the clubs, like, twenty-four-seven. I'm not even gonna say anything about your little men that you have meeting you at the gym. You can't train them all, Kendra."

Ignoring Sean lying in the bed next to her, Kendra got up, grabbed for her housecoat, and headed out of the room.

"Are you crazy? Sean is right here and could have easily heard you, Gracie," Kendra whispered angrily, walking to the lower level of their apartment. "It's not even like that. I . . . I just don't know if I'm still feeling the relationship. That's all."

"Hmm. Well, don't you think you need to talk to him about all of that? I mean, Kendra, you see me and what I'm going through with Dillian disappearing, how he kept me out of the loop. Be real about it."

"It's deeper than that, Gracie . . . and what do you really care? Don't step to me about my business when you have no idea what I'm going through . . . I," she wanted to come clean, but Gracie interrupted her.

"Nothing is deeper than having your heart ripped out of your chest by someone you love. Someone that is in love with you, Kendra. It's not fair. Do you know how I feel? Do you know what I'm going through? And you're going to take Sean through the same thing."

"It's all about you, right? It's all about Gracie, Dillian, the gym and whatever else that moves you."

Anger rose in Kendra. It was all about Gracie and always had been; one of the reasons she didn't share her problems with her friend to begin with.

"Look, I'm not about to talk to you about what's going on in my house. You wanted to know if I was going to be in tomorrow, and the answer is no. I'll call you and let you know if anything else changes. Goodnight, Gracie." Kendra hung up as she heard her best friend sobbing on the other line.

Right as she placed her car in her parking space on the side of her condo, Gracie's face flooded with pain as she realized that all of her anger for her friend was still pain she held in from Dillian. She pulled herself out of her vehicle. She said a silent prayer, fighting tears as she walked to her home.

CHAPTER EIGHTEEN

Gracie. Nothing and no one could override the thoughts that Marcus had going through his mind. Not that he hated to admit it, but he was head over heels with Gracie all over again. He felt that she was the one. She always had been.

Since getting into the groove with Gracie, Marcus had felt secure knowing that Gracie's presence was and had always been missing in his life. Not just on a significant-other level, but as a friend as well.

Back in his senior year of high school, when his parents decided to divorce, Gracie was the only person who helped him stay focused on his future. Marcus lost all hope about graduating and taking the SAT, but Gracie was the one who reminded him to study and fill out applications for college. She was there.

She never questioned his tears; she just comforted him. But most of all, Gracie helped him lean on God for understanding and to know that tomorrow would be a brighter day, and it had been. Her listening ear helped pull him through, and that's exactly what he wanted to be for her now in return for all that she had done for him. His mind was made up to be there for Gracie.

Marcus was cruising and listening to the sports radio station. He glanced at his ringing cell phone in its cradle.

"This is Marcus," he answered after he pushed the talk button.

"Hey, Marcus, it's Michelle. I was just calling to see how you were doing."

"Oh! Hey. What's going on?" Securing his hands-free earpiece, Marcus continued his drive.

"Nothing much, I didn't want us to become complete strangers, so I just thought I'd call and check on you. How's Gracie?"

Marcus didn't jump to conclusions about the last question. He just went with the flow. "Uh, she's fine."

"Really?" Michelle asked in a surprising voice, hoping she would make Marcus fall into her trap.

"Yeah really. Is that surprising?"

"Oh, it's just that, in her condition, I thought, well. . . . Oh never mind. Well let me let you go, you have a . . ."

"Wait Michelle . . . what are you talking about . . . Gracie and her condition. I don't understand?"

"Well . . ."

As Michelle told him the secret, as she knew it, about Gracie and AIDS, Marcus had to swerve to avoid hitting the compact car in the next lane.

Marcus quickly made the connection to Dillian's disappearance.

Marcus removed his left hand from the steering wheel and kept his right hand in place. With a confused look in his eyes and a nauseated stomach, Marcus yanked his earpiece out of his ear. Hitting the wheel out of disbelief and pain, all Marcus worried about was getting to Gracie.

CHAPTER NINETEEN

Gracie stood at her apartment door, yet to open it. Even with the key in the keyhole. After her strenuous day at the gym, her main focus was to get in her apartment and rest. She heard the phone ring on the other side of the door, and dropped her grocery bags to the ground. She ran into the house to answer the call. It was the automated message.

"Hello?" she answered.

Gracie listened to the beginning of the message, but then froze with fear. Gracie sat still on the edge of her sofa as to not make any unnecessary noises. Before, she hadn't noticed that message was directly meant for her. However, listening to its entirety, she knew it was indeed.

Hello, this is the Department of Health Services in your area. This message is for Gracie Gregory. It is very imperative that you contact us immediately. Our number is 1-888-555-5555. Again . . .

Why would the Health Department keep calling me? . . .
"The health department!" Now, she was nervous but
not enough to stop her from searching for an ink pen.

Gracie jotted the number down and decided to give
the department a call.

"Hi, yes this is Gracie Gregory and I'm returning a
phone call." Her thoughts got deeper, and she wondered if the phone call had actually been meant for
her. Gracie waited to be transferred to the person that
could help her.

"Thank you for holding, what time would you like to
make an appointment?"

"Oh, I'm not making an appointment. Well actually,
I would like to know the reason behind the call. Can
you let me know, please?"

With all her effort, she was still unable to get the
reason for the repeated phone call. She had no resolu-
tion and was down at the point of horror. She stood,
pacing back and forth, hoping that the representative
would give in and relieve her tension. It wasn't happening.

"Well can you at least brief me on what it is I'd be
looking forward to *if* I make the appointment? What if
you have the wrong Gracie Gregory?"

"Ms. Gregory that will be something we'll have to
deal with then. Can you please allow me to make an
appointment with you at one of our local clinics?"

"A clinic?" Gracie stopped in her tracks and demanded to know what was going on. "If you can't tell
me what's going on, let me speak to your supervisor.
I'm a busy woman and I'm not just coming down there
just to be coming, ma'am."

Gracie would have never guessed that a phone call of
such importance was actually meant for her. The super-

visor explained why it was important for her to cooperate.

"Ms. Gregory, this is procedure that cannot be broken, but what I can let you know is that your name is in a database of people who need to be contacted for testing."

When she found out what kind of testing he was talking about, she had to sit right where she was, which was on the floor. She needed to clear her name for disease testing. He went on to say, "Because it could have been any disease possibly contracted in a sexual way, you need not waste anymore time. Make an appointment right away."

Gracie made the appointment for the very next morning and disconnected the call. She dragged the groceries a few feet into the house. Then she resumed her Indian-style sitting position on the floor.

Confused about the whole conversation, Gracie was terrified by the mere thought of having a disease. Tears started to fall.

"A disease?"

Gracie prided herself in her caution to protect herself—from the first to the last time she'd had sex. There was no link on how, when, why, or where she'd contracted the disease. Then it hit her.

It was after a friend's July fourth party the previous summer that she and Dillian had one of their most romantic nights together. Once they got back to their side of town, they opened the patio doors and sat out lounging, watching the fireworks light up the sky at Fair Park in south Dallas. They shared one bottle of wine, opened another, and worked on the remainder. Before they knew it, they had forgone the fireworks and found themselves in the bed, making love without protection. Until the phone conversation with the health care worker, Gracie had placed the incident in the back of her mind.

The next morning, Gracie sat in the cold waiting area of the clinic. Minutes felt like hours. Her eyes flitted around the room, refusing to rest on any one person for too long. Instead of the patients, she took in the white walls and the plethora of posters that were taped along them; posters on high blood pressure, cancer, the flu, abortion, STDs. Just as she began to read a "WHAT TO DO IF YOU THINK YOU HAVE AN STD" poster, the receptionist told her that the doctor would see her.

Gracie clasped her hands together and wrung them. She saw stirrups and shiny metal instruments, but what really waited for her at the end of the hall was a counselor and an office. A petite white woman in a fitted brown blazer guided her to the office, and her nervousness turned to fear. She began to think that this "disease" was more than a case of chlamydia.

With all of her strength, Gracie paced herself with her too many thoughts. She walked toward an open seat and sat impatiently, waiting to get to the reason for the visit.

Gracie sat face to face with Sandy, the clinics counselor and immediately started her questioning.

"Can you please tell me why I'm here?" Gracie asked.

"Yes. We'll get to that. Did anyone accompany you today, Ms. Gregory?"

Gracie let the woman know that she was indeed

alone. The look on the counselor's face took Gracie's helpless fear up a notch.

"Can you please just let me know what the problem is? I've waited all night long."

For the next twenty minutes, Gracie sat and listened to this stranger tell her that another stranger turned her name into the health department because of the possibility that a disease had been transferred from his body to hers. Nothing could have taken the look of helplessness off of Gracie's face when she found out the infection was the infection of them all: HIV.

"Gracie . . . Gracie . . ."

Gracie was blocked in her own world, in her own nightmare. It wasn't until Sandy got up from behind her desk, came around to Gracie, and shook her that Gracie responded.

Gracie answered Sandy's questions with head nods and sat crying with her head in her lap. She thought of her whole life in her first visit to the clinic. Every time she would try not to think about the worst, she felt she couldn't neglect reality.

No, she moved her head slowly to answer if she had had any transfusions, drug use. *No,* she moved her head when asked if she had or had had unprotected sex, was she promiscuous. Gracie was stumped.

Gracie agreed to take the test to determine if her lifestyle would indeed change. Crying with every emotion present, Gracie thought she would fall dead right on the clinic's floor when Sandy asked if she wanted to call anyone to pick her up.

"No! I'm sorry. That's not possible. I live alone and I don't have any immediate family around this way." Gracie knew that she could call her godparents for anything. That realization stopped her breathing. *This could change the lives of everyone I love*, Gracie thought. With that thought, her tears started all over again.

"Momma," she muttered.

"I'm sorry?" Sandy asked.

Looking up for the first time, Gracie thought about her parents out loud. "Tell me what to do, what do I say . . . where do I go. I mean, there has to be something done, right? When can I get my results? I need to know, ma'am!"

The counselor wrapped her arms around her client. Another young woman lost, fighting, not knowing where her fate lay. Not knowing if her cries would cease or increase for years to come.

CHAPTER TWENTY

Gracie loosened her hair with one yank of her ponytail holder hoping to relieve the physical pain between her ears. Nothing could erase the pain; not aspirin, not releasing the ponytail holder, not pressing her temples with her hands, not even her pleas to God at the moment. The pain consumed her. Ever since she found out about the possibility of contracting HIV, Gracie had locked herself in her apartment and tried to understand her situation. It was official: she didn't and couldn't understand. At least nothing she wanted to understand.

Except when she tried to call Kendra, Gracie hadn't spoken to a single being and didn't plan on it. How could she? There was no way possible she could hold a conversation without breaking down. Gracie couldn't bring herself to believe that all was good and that there was a chance she could test negative. She was always optimistic but she wouldn't allow herself to be in denial about the one time without protection. She wouldn't even let herself off the hook about continuous pre-martial sex, altogether. In her mind, no matter who gave her what, it had been her own fault for even crossing the boundary of sex before marriage.

Sandy, the counselor, had cautioned Gracie not to get her hopes up . . . but also, to not lose her hope. Even when Gracie told her about the one time she and Dillian had neglected to use protection, Sandy's advice was to wait and see.

Wait and see, huh? Gracie thought to herself as she finally rolled out of her king-sized bed. She stumbled a few feet on her way to the door and collapsed into a heap on the floor. Just like the previous night, Gracie's mind played every inch of her life before her eyes. This time, without trying to fight it, Gracie wallowed in her fears.

"How could he do this to me?" she screamed. She knew in her heart, her gut, that the *anonymous* person was Dillian. It hurt her to her soul to think that Dillian could keep something like this from her. They had been so careful, so very careful, making sure to always use protection. One fragment of a moment in which passion overrode common sense could be the difference between a healthy life and one of medication and declining health.

Gracie crawled to the door and used the knob to hoist herself up. Her sobs shook her body uncontrollably and made her steps unsteady as she stepped out into the hallway. Her knees buckled and she backed into the corner of the hallway to remain standing.

"Lord," Gracie said, in a voice so full of sorrow that she knew God would have to hear her, "this is hard! I know that you are with me everyday and every step that I have to take, but I need you to pull me through this trial! I don't know if asking you to help me through this makes me selfish, but you said if I should ask

something in your name, it would be done. Lord, I
need for your will to be done in my life."

Gracie was in pain. Her head boomed, heart ached,
and she couldn't stop gagging. She knew she would have
vomited had she eaten anything. Unable to make it to
the kitchen for food, Gracie crawled back into bed and
pulled the covers up around her head. Every time her
eyes closed and the darkness came over her, Gracie
thought of the people that mattered in her life. She
curled into the fetal position and rocked as she thought
about her parents having to bury her instead of the
other way around.

"That's just how it goes," she said out loud in a
weak, nervous voice. "You do *almost* everything right
just to end up with pain in the end. Does my 'almost'
count, God? Does it?"

Gracie worked so hard to keep stress away from her
parents. It didn't look like it was going to pay off after
all. Now she would bring them the ultimate pain she
felt a child could bring their parents. She worried if
her parents would turn against her. She liked to think
not, but she also knew that HIV could tear apart some
of the closest families, so why would hers be spared?

Gracie searched deep for assurance that her family
had her back. She remembered her last visit to Paris
and sitting in her parents' dining room as her mother
gave solid, loving advice. That told Gracie that they
wouldn't turn their backs on her for anything. Gracie
fought the urge to pick up the phone and call her parents for the support she so desperately needed. Even
now, she peeked from under the covers at her nightstand, staring at the cordless phone. Though she whispered "no," her hand said yes. She snatched the phone
from the stand and began to dial, only to find someone
already on the other end.

"Marcus?"

"Hello, Gracie," he said. "Is that you?"

"Uh, Marcus; yes, it's me." Gracie cleared her throat and sat up in her bed, hoping to disguise the anguish in her voice. "How are you?"

"I'm good, Gracie. The question is, how are you? I've been trying to get in contact with you for almost two days. Where have you been?"

"I've been here. Sorry I haven't returned your call, but I've been busy talking to different site managers. As a matter of fact, I was about to make another call. Can I call you back?"

"Well, actually, Gracie, since you're not on the phone yet, I just want to see how you're doing." He wanted and needed to know more. "Gracie, is something wrong? I mean, is there anything you need to tell me about Dillian and why he *really* left you? Just tell me."

"What?" After seconds of silence, Gracie knew she had to get off the phone. "Don't be silly, Marcus. Look, let me call you back." Without waiting for a response, Gracie disconnected the phone and forgot all about her call to her parents. That was all it took for her to fall.

Deeper and deeper she fell into her self pity. Hearing Marcus's voice only brought on more worries. Now she was doubly confused. Had she given the virus to Dillian? If so, how? And besides that, how in the world did Marcus know, and who else knew?

She had no idea what she was going to tell Marcus for him to move on with his life. They'd already been hot and heavy, close enough for her to rub her virus off on him, but thankfully, she had found willpower. And how would she keep him away forever without letting him know everything? If Marcus found out all details, she just knew he would most certainly leave her.

Thoughts of her parents and Marcus infiltrated Gracie's mind, but there was still enough room for self pity. She resigned herself to being single forever, not having children or being a mother. When she thought about her love for children, Gracie felt her chest cave in. She replayed her moral standard of being married before having children. She cursed herself for trying to halfway do the right thing. Maybe that was why she was in the bind now . . . halfway living right.

Gracie rose to her feet. Without knowing her next move, she walked over to her vanity mirror and angrily knocked every item off with one swipe of her hand. Frustration and anger shot through her whole being as she thought of Dillian and the secret he had kept from her.

"Why'd you do this to me? Lord, why did you let this happen to me?"

With her mind in a whirl, Gracie raced to the closet, the same one that held most of the things Dillian had given her. She came across a framed picture of the two, flung it across the room, and watched it crack and shatter against the wall. She cut her fingers on the shards of glass as she ran and ripped the picture from the frame and tore the picture into thin, long strips.

Not even close to being finished, Gracie went through the apartment finding pictures of her and Dillian and slammed them against the wall. Thinking in the moment only, Gracie raced up to a walled decorative mirror and began hitting it with her closed and bleeding fist until it fell to the floor, leaving large, piercing slates of glass.

Gracie fell to the floor, not caring if the debris cut her or not. She eyed the largest and sharpest weapon grabbed it, and held on tight.

"Does it matter? Look at me! Look at what I've become," she cried out to her lonely apartment while gripping tighter to the piece of mirror. "Who's gonna want to share a life with me? I don't even want to be me!" With a loud and shrill cry, Gracie only half-thought her next move.

Gracie didn't know what she wanted to do with the broken glass, but she knew she wanted to see what was going to kill her. Blood. When the blood began to flow down her palms and down her forearms, Gracie's cries reached a peak. Subconsciously, she went for her wrists.

Not thinking about her parents, not thinking about her gym, not thinking about Marcus or the children she one day wanted to have. Forsaking God's promises and God's words, Gracie hollered out as she drove the piercing glass into her skin.

It had to be a dream. The phone calls, the messages, and even reality. Her eyes opened only on reflex. Gracie turned and looking around her room, her eyes taking in the disarray. Finally seeing her alarm clock, Gracie's sight landed on the neon green numbers that displayed 12:29 a.m. She was groggy on the floor beside her bed. She had no memory of ever leaving the living area, Gracie's thoughts on suicide just hours before had been over ridden by her ability to unconsciously cry herself to sleep.

The glass wouldn't go as deep as Gracie had intended for it to go. Yes there would be a surface scar, but God heals all. Gracie found the strength in knowing that God kept His word. He was always with her . . . through her good times and her bad. Knowing that God wouldn't be pleased with her giving up, Gracie brought back her remembrance, the fear of the Lord, and strength was given.

Guilt wedged into Gracie's heart. She was embarrassed by her suicidal thoughts. Regardless, No one was happier to be alive than Gracie. The way she would possibly have to live bothered her. Quickly looking over at the clock, praises rushed out of Gracie's mouth as she found strength in her weakest hour. The something for which she had been looking came into her being.

"Late in the midnight hour . . . Lord, I thank you!" Gracie mouthed the words that she had heard her pastor quote time after time about how God can turn things around in the midnight hour. Gracie stood slowly to her feet and praised God even with her lack of energy. The devil lost his battle and she was full of praise.

With her lazy vocal thanks and praises to God, Gracie allowed her revelation of everything "being all right" to dance around in her soul. It was still hard to swallow, but just the thoughts of being able to breathe, walk, and talk were very precious commodities to Gracie.

Still physically weak, she climbed in bed and rested with her new strength on her mind.

CHAPTER TWENTY-ONE

Though Gracie awakened to an uncertain day later in the morning, she found the strength to eat, drink, cook, and clean. She even had courage to talk to the outside world. She wasn't ready to let her family in on her ordeal, but she at least was ready for the results, or so she thought.

Gracie sucked in a deep breath and picked up the phone, quickly dialing the clinic's number. She paced the floor as the phone rang.

"I can do this," she whispered to the quiet of her apartment. Her fingers gripped the receiver, and just as she was about to chicken out and hang up, someone answered. "Dallas County Health Department, can you please hold?" Gracie responded by hanging up. She wasn't ready to hear the answer to her fate.

She stared at the receiver in her hand. It was Friday. If she didn't do it now, she would have to wait until Monday. Christmas was on Tuesday. Gracie solemnly wondered what would be God's gift to her this year.

Christmas was a holiday usually spent with her mother and father back home. But Gracie didn't have the energy to leave her bedroom, let alone get in her car and drive to Paris.

Gracie picked the cordless phone back up and dialed her parents' number. It was time to connect with the real world, and there were none more real than her mother and father.

She sat in a cross-legged position on her bed. Gracie barely had enough time to take in a breath before her father picked up the phone and yelled, "Gracie, where on earth have you been?" So much for caller-ID.

"Daddy," Gracie responded as she rubbed her forehead. "I've been here. Look, I'm sorry I haven't returned any phone calls, but—

"What were you thinking? You know how your mother likes to worry. Everyone from Kendra to Marcus has called down here looking for you. What's going on with you?" In the background Gracie could hear her mother asking if that was her run-away daughter.

She let out an emotional sigh and fell back on her many pillows. Gracie wished she could erase everything up to this point, but she couldn't. She knew she should have been in contact with her parents, if no one else, but her situation had her trapped in her own mind. She definitely hadn't been in control.

"Daddy, I know I owe everyone an explanation, but the only people that matter right now are you and Momma. I need to talk to you two, but I just don't have the energy to drive down. Can you two come up here for Christmas instead of me coming down?"

"Let me talk to her when you finish Jacob . . . she know I'm mad!" her mother said in the background.

Shushing his wife, Jacob felt the weariness in Gracie's voice. "What's wrong, Gracie? You always come home for Christmas. What's going on?"

"What's wrong, Jacob?" Mrs. Gregory demanded.

"Daddy, I know. I just need to be here to take care of personal things, and I need you two here with me."

Gracie felt one of her many boulders remove itself from her shoulders as she talked to her parents and they agreed to come to Dallas. Even though the talk wasn't in as much detail as she had hoped, Gracie knew she could always count on her parents to love her and put her at ease.

"Well, girlie whatever you need, just let us know and we'll do it. We'll be glad to come down for Christmas, honey."

After talking to both of her parents, Gracie resolved to get up and do something. She settled in at her built-in desk in her room with plenty of paperwork in tow, including her living will that she planned on changing before nightfall.

However, Gracie's work mood evaporated as she sat down and turned on her CD player with Lashun Pace's "God is Faithful" blasting through the speakers. Tears streamed down her face before she could get started on her mission. She had done so much with her life. Some good and some questionable; yet and still, God had been faithful through it all. Deep within, she knew that God meant for her to meet Him through this new pain. She knew that He already knew her steps before she did and it would all be settled in His will.

She was so proud of her accomplishments: the fitness center that she started from scratch and the second center that would put her over the top. The mere thought of both made her mind and heart crash, as she knew she would be turning her dream over to Kendra.

It wasn't that Kendra couldn't handle it; it was the thought of giving her baby away.

She sat in a trance with pen in hand. Gracie was startled by the doorbell which was followed by a knock at the door. She raced into the kitchen and eyed the small circuit TV that was linked to the remote camera at her doorway. It was a sick Kendra, blowing her nose, leaning against the door, and looking as if she was about to camp out in front of the door if Gracie didn't open it first.

Gracie gave in. She couldn't stay locked up forever, nor could she let her anger at her friend's recent behavior linger. Especially with her parents coming into town the following day, people would know she was there. Gracie accepted defeat and opened the door.

"I knew you were in here." Kendra barged her way through the door, her hands on her hips. "Where have you been?" She started in, not even alluding to the last conversation they had had.

Gracie realized that her hibernation had worried everyone in her life. She stepped back and Kendra entered further inside.

"Didn't you get my message?" Referring to the message that was left close to four days earlier, Gracie still didn't feel like company.

"Uh yes," Kendra replied. "Did you get *my* message? Well, messages?" Before she went on with her rant, she saw Gracie's bandaged hand. "Girl, what happened to your hand?"

Kendra came in close and took Gracie's hand into hers. She began to remove the bandages when Gracie pulled her hand back quickly.

"No!" Gracie yelled. "You can't!" Knowing her status wasn't certain, Gracie wouldn't dare put her friend in danger.

Kendra tilted her head to the side and looked at Gracie as if she had lost her mind.

"Okay, okay," she said, raising her hands in surrender. "Gracie, you act as if I have never taken care of your wounds before; we both have. Dang, just because I have a cold . . ."

Gracie remembered all the times in college when she or Kendra came in with scraped knees or bruises from track and hurdles. Who needed a doctor when she had her best friend? Still, Gracie couldn't risk harming Kendra.

"I'm sorry," Gracie said. "It's just that it hurts, and I barely want to touch it myself. Actually, I'm fine though, other than just needing rest." Gracie slipped her bandaged hand behind her back and added, "Look at you! You're the one that should be in bed."

Kendra opened her mouth to talk, but coughed instead. "I'm going," she said, a sneeze interrupting the words. "Now that I know that you're okay."

"Well yeah, I'm fine. How's the gym?"

"It's holding up. Did I tell you that Miss Prissy stopped coming to the gym all together? She must be mad as heck at you. Oh and get this . . . she's not happy with the workout and she wants her money back. She went on and on about the fine print and how to get out of the contract. Yada, yada, yada."

"Just reimburse her," Gracie said, waving a hand in the air as if to dismiss Michelle. "I have more to deal with than her. You want tea?"

"No, I'm going to get going." Kendra gave Gracie a small hug before walking to the door. When she opened it, she turned back and faced Gracie. "Don't be a stranger, girl. When you feel better, I want the *real* deal on what's been going on. Because you know I know you . . . love ya, girl."

Gracie watched the door close. She stood there, hugging herself, wanting to tell her best friend about the pain that welled up inside of her. Badly in need of a shoulder to lean on, even for just a moment, Gracie fought against her will to open the door and yell out for Kendra. Instead, she just stood to be her own support.

That night, Gracie read her Bible in bed. She let the words soak into her soul, and she understood each and every word. She knew it was okay to cry with emotion. She knew that after the tears and the mourning, it was time to move on.

No problem was too big for God. No heartache was too deep for God. None. Gracie knew that the only way to get over a problem was to give it to Him, but she wasn't able to *leave* it with Him. Not yet. She felt it just wasn't time or He would have said so.

Getting down on her knees in front of her bed, Gracie prayed with strength, a prayer to leave her worries with the Lord, and she did. She had a special connection with God that she had not put to work since she had gotten the news. Years ago, Gracie realized she had "it." She could sense the answers to questions that she had asked God. They had a relationship and the only problem was that she hadn't been devoted enough to know that all God needed was for her to open up and lean on Him.

"Lord, I'm yours. Whatever you want from me, whatever you need from me, whoever you need me to connect with . . . God, I'm yours. I repent my sins to you, Father. I have sinned and I cannot even begin to ask why. Here I am, give me strength through this trial so that I may, in the end, do your Will."

There was no doubt in Gracie's mind that God's answer would prevail in her life. Whatever He wanted, needed her to do, she was willing. Yes, it would require her to give her whole being, which He made, back to Him, but at this very point in her life, that alone would be no challenge. She needed God and she hoped He wanted her.

CHAPTER TWENTY-TWO

Her parents made it into town that Saturday night. Gracie sat them down two hours later, after their short rest and explained her situation to them. They took the news exactly like she had thought they would. They hurt for her.

Her parents sat on the sofa opposite from her, fighting through tears as she talked with no energy. Gracie exhaled a deep breath, waiting for a response from her two supporters.

Her mother responded first. She halfway ran over to Gracie and comforted her in her arms. Her dad stayed in his seat and searched for words. He couldn't move; he knew that his legs wouldn't be able to hold his emotional frame.

"Girlie . . . uh . . . I don't know what to say. Are you okay, your life, umm? Is there anything . . . umm?"

Mr. Gregory, a big man who never shed tears in front of his daughter, was now sobbing uncontrollably. He always wanted to be the strong one in his family, to be there for "his girls" no matter what, but the unpredicted news tore him up. The words, questions he had for Gracie couldn't even settle on his lips before he swallowed them whole. Putting his head in his hands, Mr. Gregory couldn't look in Gracie's direction. He knew that there wasn't anything he could do for her. This battle was one that he hadn't even anticipated.

Mrs. Gregory placed one kiss on Gracie's cheek, her tears matching her daughter's. Mrs. Gregory released her daughter only to console her husband. "Now, Jacob, it's going to be . . ." She hadn't thought that she would break down along with her husband. Mrs. Gregory kneeled on the floor in front of him and embraced him as they cried together.

Mrs. Gregory stayed in her position, frozen with horror, holding her husband. She didn't feel her own tears that had rolled down her aging, but well-kept face. Several times, she'd stopped her mind from fast-forwarding to the end, but she couldn't keep her hurt inside. Remembering that death was the end to HIV on television programs, Mrs. Gregory saw an end for her daughter.

"Lord, no! Lord, why?" Mrs. Gregory cried.

Mrs. Gregory didn't know much about the disease, but knowing that her baby girl could be in pain before she left the world was enough to break her heart.

"I just don't get it . . . I just don't get it, Lord! Why my baby?"

Wiping the tears from her wet face, Gracie walked over to her parents who took her into their circle. As soon as one would calm down, the emotions ran through the next one's veins. It went on like that several hours.

"Momma, I know . . . I'm sorry! I don't want to take

y'all through this. I'm sorry!" Gracie cried in fear.
"Please forgive me. I didn't mean to bring this to you,
but I don't have anyone else."

"It's okay, baby girl. It's not your fault. Lord, help us,
please! Help our baby, Lord!" Mrs. Gregory cried out.

"Baby don't you dare think that we don't want to
walk this walk with you. You're our baby, Gracie . . .
you're still our special baby no matter what. You
hear?" Her dad said sternly as tears crowded his eyes.

They rocked, moaned, cried, and loved each other for
whatever it was worth until they had gained enough
strength to pull themselves together . . . for the time
being, anyway. They knew it wasn't going to be easy,
but they searched and found strength.

Later, after everyone's emotions had settled, Gracie
explained the changes she would have to go through if
she was positive. She elaborated a bit on the medications and withdrawals and so forth. It was hard to be
strong in front of her parents when all Gracie wanted
to do was cry and sleep.

She was embarrassed to have to tell them how it
was slightly possible that she wouldn't be infected
with HIV. There was a slight relief in her parents'
eyes. Although they knew abstinence was best, they
were glad to hear that she had used protection.

"See, I know God can make a way," Mrs. Gregory
said. "So, honey, we are just going to believe that God
will bless you. You know He's still in the blessing business, and don't you forget that!"

When Gracie heard, "no matter what, we still love
you," she knew she could make it through the storm
with the strength from God and the love from her parents. No one scolded her with "should've" messages, only
support and love. It rested in Gracie's overwhelmed
and damaged heart.

* * *

On Sunday morning, Gracie held hands with her parents as they listened to a church sermon on faith. Gracie had always tried to live by faith. Recently, she found it hard to believe in, but yet she was fighting for it. Sitting between her folks, Gracie felt her parents' love emanate from them to her. This along with the sermon, bought tears to her eyes. The tears eventually slipped down her cheeks.

Faith comes by hearing and hearing by the word of God. That was the first scripture that Gracie had ever learned. She had kept it dear to her heart. It was her inspiration through college and in the stressful first years of her business. Faith meant something more to her. Without it, she felt she couldn't be positive and prosperous in her life. The sermon from the pulpit jumped out at Gracie. She knew that it was going to take faith for her to overcome.

"Open up to God . . . believe God. People, whatever you need from the Lord believe it! Receive it! Have faith and hold onto God's unchanging hand . . ." Reverend Darsey told the congregation.

Knowing that the sermon was given to her from God, Gracie's bones shook as she felt the Spirit moving in her. She knew she would have to stand fast in her faith, even if she received the news that she was HIV positive. The reality of that pained her, but she knew no matter what, God was still in control. That's when the real test would come. With tears flowing, Gracie knew that all the trials of the previous week could only have been the beginning.

All and all, even with her slight optimism, Gracie needed support behind her. Like in the scripture her mother had given her to read the night before, *"now faith is the substance of things hoped for, the evidence of things not seen.*" She found that miracles were the evidence of faith. It all became clear.

When she was just a little girl, Gracie remembered the preacher saying to never underestimate one's prayers to God. With the prayers, you have to have faith that things will come to past. With that thought, she spoke her hopes into existence.

"Lord, I believe you! Lord, I love you!" Gracie joined the congregation and stood up. She raised her wet eyes toward heaven. She asked that God's will be done completely in her life. Although Gracie wanted desperately for her results to come back negative, she refused to harp on the results. Either way, she asked to remain healthy and move in the direction that *He* wanted her to go.

She released her worries to God. Gracie knew she wasn't the only one praying for her when she felt her parents' hands on her back. They comforted her and prayed that healing would seep into her body through their hands, God's anointed hands.

When Rebecca heard the voice on the other end of the phone, her breath caught in her throat. It had been so long since she heard her brother's voice, she couldn't get her hopes up.

"Dillian?" she asked into the phone, her voice high and shrill. "Dillian, is that you? Where are you? Are you okay?"

Tears spilled from her eyes. She could hear Dillian sniffling.

"It's me, Becky," Dillian said, breaking the silence. "I'm in the hospital."

"Hospital? What are you talking about, D? Which hospital are you at? I'm on my way."

"I'm at Baylor, sis, but you don't have to rush down. I have something I need to tell you first, okay?"

"Okay. What? I'm listening, D, go ahead."

Dillian paused; the words stuck in his jaw. "I'm sick."

"Sick? Okay. Sick like what? You're scaring me!"

"I have HIV, Becky."

"Oh no! Dillian, don't tell me that!" With no response from her brother, Rebecca let out a heart-wrenching scream. "Dillian, no! What do you mean?"

"Yes, Becky, it's true, and I'm sorry for springing this on you like this. I swear I am. From what the doctors are saying, since I'm not taking the medication properly, my immune system is weakening. I'll be in here for a while."

"I'm on my way, D," Rebecca said through her tears. "Do you want me to get Momma and bring her with me so you can tell her?"

"You go ahead and tell her and see if she wants to come or not."

"Okay."

"Have you talked to Gracie?" Dillian asked.

"My Lord!" Rebecca felt the oxygen seep from her brain as she grew faint. She sat. She thought about the disease being passed to Gracie. She cried out again. "I'll call her too. She's been looking for you."

"No. That's something I'll have to do. Thanks, Becky."

After hanging up, Dillian tried to pray. He had given up on himself, and he never once thought about praying or asking God to help him. He closed his eyes tight and opened his mouth to speak, but no words would come out. He still felt helpless. He had given up on the idea that he could fight this disease. Several failed attempts later, Dillian gave up trying to pray and picked up the phone. He still had one more person to talk to, someone he loved and who didn't deserve what he was about to place upon her.

"I tell you," Gracie's mother said as the trio entered Gracie's apartment. "There's nothing like a good sermon to make you feel wonderful inside."

"You got that right," Gracie's father agreed.

Gracie dropped her purse onto the sofa and noticed the answering machine blinking on the end table.

"I'll be right back," Gracie told her parents, who were still discussing the sermon. "I'm going to check my messages." Gracie began listening to her awaiting messages as she walked to her room.

Gracie walked into her bedroom and sat on the edge of the bed. There were three messages. One was from Kendra, who called to check up on her. Another was a daily message left by Marcus, who finally said he was coming over after church no matter what she said. The third . . . the third made Gracie's body go rigid. It was Dillian. Her mouth dropped open and she stopped breathing to hear the message clearly.

"Gracie, this is Dillian. I'm not sure if you know by now, but I'm in the hospital. I wish you were there so that I could talk directly to you while I have the nerve . . . but . . . Oh, well. The answer to the question I'm sure you've been asking yourself over and over, is yes, I'm HIV positive . . ."

Nothing . . . nothing at all could stop Gracie from dropping to her knees to fight her invisible pain. To actually hear the words come from his mouth, it was now evident that Dillian had been the one behind her whole dilemma. She eased her shoes off with one hand while the other covered her opened mouth. Gracie scooted herself backward until she was hidden behind her closet's door.

In her closet, Gracie held her heart and rocked herself. Her mind wandered from the church service to her parents in the other room to her appointment at the clinic. With her mouth open, tears fell into her clasped hands and she prayed to God, asking Him to keep her mind. She fell back onto the floor and and cried until sleep covered her, followed by peace.

CHAPTER TWENTY-THREE

Marcus moped around Sunday after church as he waited for a return call from Gracie. It never came. When he became suspicious enough to consider going to her apartment, he voted against it. He had never been one to crowd anyone who didn't want to be crowded.

He thought things were different with him and Gracie this time around. They were growing in their new-found friendship with several dates and long conversations to show for it. Even though he knew some things about Gracie's private life, Marcus left those thoughts way in the back of his mind.

Gracie's conversations had always been pleasing to him. He didn't know if he had done the right thing by hinting at her private life, but he felt that he had a right to know. That is, if they were going to be involved. Because of her reaction to the question, Marcus had a great deal of worry.

HIV wasn't something one could take lightly. On one hand, he was glad she didn't return any of his calls because he needed time to think about whether the rumor was true. On the other, he wanted to be a friend no matter what the circumstances were.

In his heart, Gracie was always number one. Their time apart had done nothing to make him feel different. Even when she had given him his walking papers and told him that she couldn't do it any longer, all he asked was for her to keep an open spot in her heart for him. By the looks of it, she had.

Whether she knew it or not, Gracie meant a great deal to him. In their earlier years, she had loved him like a woman should love a man, even when the man still clung to his childish ways. Not one time did she change for him, or ask him to change for her, and that is exactly what Marcus admired about her. If she said that she wasn't going to do something, she didn't. If she said she would do something, she did it. Gracie was the type of woman who didn't sit around waiting for a man to change. She moved on if he wasn't ready. However, she wasn't too stiff against giving one a second chance once he matured.

Gracie had also given him the little knowledge he had about spirituality. Not religion, but understanding and having a relationship with God. Before Gracie, Marcus only prayed before he ate his meals and that was because he caught on from his early school years. Initially, he had followed Gracie in her pursuit of God because he liked her. But then the whole spirituality life became interesting to him. He gave in to God and didn't give up after he and Gracie broke up.

By Sunday evening, Marcus had every intention to grab his coat and head over to her apartment. Only he was stopped by Michelle in his doorway.

"Oh!" Michelle yelled. She threw her hand up to her chest. "You scared me. I was just about to ring the doorbell. Are you going out somewhere?"

"What are you doing here, Michelle? Was I expecting you?" he asked sarcastically.

Marcus stared hard at Michelle, angry that she would just show up without being invited. It made him second guess his trip to Gracie's. He leaned against the door with no intention of welcoming her in.

"No silly. You weren't, but I just had some news that I wanted to share with you and was sure I could help you out." She batted her eyes under her permanent makeup-filled eyebrows.

With a far off look on his face, Marcus said, "Help me out? What are you talking about?"

"Well, can I come in and talk to you, or are you in a big hurry?"

Marcus stepped back, and hesitantly let Michelle in. He would let her have her say, and then he would be on his way. He followed Michelle into the living room and watched her take a seat. He remained standing.

"So what's up, Michelle?" he asked.

"Okay," she answered, sighing. "Just so you're not kept waiting, you know the rumor I told you about, regarding Dillian and Gracie?"

Marcus rolled his eye and crossed his arms over his chest. "Yes, I know," he replied, irritated.

"Well, it has been confirmed and I have paperwork that proves that Dillian is in the hospital because of complications with HIV. My sources are telling me that he is pretty much in denial and won't take his meds. I'm here because I'm sure you're going to want to press charges against Gracie for not letting you in on her little sickness. Most definitely, if the woman is sleeping around and possibly infecting people, it's against the law and on your behalf . . ."

Marcus threw his hand up, stopping Michelle in mid-sentence. For the life of him, he could not understand Michelle. Was she so hard up to win him over that she stooped to conjuring up private information on a person just so she could get next to him? Not flattered at all, the more she talked, the hotter he became under his collar. He wanted nothing more than to grab Michelle by the arm and toss her out of his apartment, but he never disrespected ladies. Even if he wanted to, he wouldn't be bold enough to do it now.

Michelle stood with well-practiced concern in her eyes. She reached out to comfort Marcus. She thought this had to be a painful and upsetting time for him. Michelle was rudely awakened from her demented dream. She opened her arms, thinking Marcus would come into them, but he pushed his arms out and backed away from her.

"Whoa! Michelle? Are you crazy or something? I mean who does this type of stuff? If Gracie knew of any sort of thing," he said, "believe me, she would have told me. There is no way she would intentionally do anything to harm me. I'm tired of hearing your headline gossip. You have to go!"

"Gossip? How do you know *she's* not lying?" Michelle tilted her head. "Maybe she's still bitter over the relationship you guys had years ago." Michelle noticed Marcus's defensive stance and tried to ease toward him. "Look, Marcus, I'm just trying to look out for your well-being. I mean, I don't want anything to happen to you. Why can't I be concerned about you?" she asked as she allowed their bodies to meet.

Michelle managed briefly to slip her arms around Marcus's neck. He took her hands and removed them once again. He picked up her bag, held her by the elbow, and escorted her out the front door. She stood staring at him, confusion, anger, and embarrassment etched into her face.

"Let this be the last time you try to come between me and Gracie," Marcus said in the strongest voice he could find while pushing her bag into her arms. "Just for the record, no matter what Gracie is going through, I'm going to be there for her. You should find you some place to be."

Marcus slammed the door and walked back into the living room, where he plopped down onto the sofa. The documents Michelle had brought along with her were on the coffee table. He reached for it and flipped through the pages. It seemed to be legitimate. For a second, a wave of nausea ran through Marcus. Nausea from Michelle's cruelty to investigate something so private in a person's life. The nausea was also about Gracie and the possibility that she too could be infected.

The whole episode left Marcus drained. He thought about what he had told Michelle, that he would be there for Gracie through her trials, but he didn't even have a second to think things through. No doubt he would be there for her, if she allowed him. But he wondered if it would be a good idea to go forward with an intimate relationship. So many questions were in his mind that they gave him an instant headache. He couldn't understand why God had allowed Gracie to resurface in his life and then let it all be for naught.

All the questions that crowded in Marcus's head needed answers. He jumped to his feet without giving himself enough time to change his mind and grabbed his coat. He prayed that he wasn't too late for Sunday evening's service at his church. Church was the best place for him.

CHAPTER TWENTY-FOUR

Not one to take rejection lightly, Michelle sat in her car not even a block away from Marcus's home. She threw her next plan into action.

"Stupid men and their stupid ways. Here I am, educated and successful with nothing hindering me and this *man* wants something that's going to kill him. Huh! He don't believe the hype, I'll bring the hype to him."

She retrieved her cellular phone from her oversized, overpriced designer bag and ran down the list of numbers in her phone until she got to her assistant.

"Marilyn? What? Yes, of course this is Michelle," she replied with aggression. "Look I need you to get the telephone number to Dillian McNab's hospital room at Parkland or Baylor . . . whichever one he's at. Better yet, find out the room number. I'll pay him a visit myself." After a breath, Michelle allowed her assistant to respond.

"I thought the files were pretty much all you needed me to locate for you. Shouldn't we get a clearance before we take things further?" Marilyn spoke slowly in hopes that Michelle wouldn't get angry because of her work ethics.

"Look, if the files were all I needed, would I be calling you telling you how to do your job? You do remember your job don't you?"

Knowing that Michelle would replace her in a heartbeat, Marilyn added some cheer to her response. "Uh. Yes, I know my job."

"Then do it," an angry and contemptuous Michelle demanded as she ended the call. "If I want something done, I see I have to get it done myself."

Michelle pushed her brake and moved the gear into drive. She figured that she had nothing better to do at the moment than to follow a wide-nosed Marcus, who was exiting his house.

Making sure she stayed her distance, Michelle slung curse after curse into the midst. She called Gracie all but Satan's wife.

She was born with the mind of an attorney, and she dominated the field. Michelle figured she'd just cut to the chase and instead of wondering where Marcus was headed, just call and ask.

"Yes, Michelle?" Marcus answered, letting out a long sigh.

She figured he couldn't be completely angry. If so, he wouldn't have answered the phone.

"Yeah, Marcus. I just wanted to call and apologize. Maybe I'm just being a bit protective of you. I hope you forgive me."

"Actually, I forgave you the first time you tried to push Gracie's business off on me. But I'd rather just end this conversation now," Marcus said as he drove four cars ahead of her on 635, LBJ Freeway. "There really isn't much more we should *ever* discuss about Gracie . . . or Dillian for that matter."

Knowing that she didn't have any more evidence for him right at the moment, she agreed. "You're right. I totally agree. Are you still at home, would you like to meet up and have tea at the new tea shop uptown?"

"No, thank you. I'm actually on my way to church service. If you'd like to accompany me there, then that's fine. Otherwise, I'll take an indefinite rain check," he said, hoping that she'd get the hint and never call him again.

"Hmm. Maybe next time. Goodbye, Marcus."

She took the first exit she saw. Michelle knew there was no getting back to Marcus. She figured she'd just cut her losses. There was no way she was going to follow him to church when there was an investigation to complete. Marcus may not have been interested, but now it was the principle of the matter. Gracie had stepped in and cut her out of Marcus's life. Now she had to return the favor.

CHAPTER TWENTY-FIVE

With her mother and father, Gracie made her way through the clinic's door. She had made sure she was the very first appointment of the day. She hoped to see the counselor and get the news she had come for.

All three had swollen eyes and trembling hands. They remained silent in the waiting area. The uneasy churning of their stomachs could be heard amid the silence of the clinic. A door opened and a counselor stood in its entranceway.

"Miss Gregory," the counselor said. No emotion was in her voice and her face was as blank as freshly fallen snow.

Gracie and her parents stood, but before they walked through the door, the counselor touched Gracie's shoulder and asked, "Are you sure you want your parents to be with you when you hear the results?"

"I'm sure," Gracie said, nodding. "I need all the support I can get. They are all I have."

She felt like a dead woman walking. Gracie tried to focus her mind on more positive thoughts like the child that she wanted in the future. The one she would give birth to. Her mind was moved to birth instead of death.

In the counselor's office, Gracie's parents kissed her cheeks. Gracie and her mother sat in the chairs that faced the desk while her dad stood behind them, his thick hands on their shoulders.

Gracie was slightly shaken when Sandy, the counselor, reached her pale hands across her desk, to Gracie and her mother.

"Let us all bow our heads, if you don't mind," Sandy whispered to the trio before her.

Gracie and her mother clasped Sandy's hands and bowed their heads.

"Heavenly Father, I come to ask you for guidance to help your dear daughter through whatever lies before her. I ask you to work through me, Lord, to be of comfort to Gracie and her family in this time of need. Bless us in this room with peace and comfort . . ."

Sandy didn't ask God for anything more than strength and for His will to be done. She prayed with anointing that could come from none other than the Lord. Her words of prayer let the Gregorys know that they were not dealing with a beginner, but with a praying woman. The prayer that went forward from the counselor put a refreshing calm over their nervousness.

As the counselor's prayer came to a close and their *amen*'s and *thank you Lord*'s rifted into the air, Gracie's father took over and began his own prayer.

"And Lord, we know that whatever you allow to happen, it's in your will. We thank you now in advance for whatever you have in store for our baby. Lord, I know that you're worthy, and for that, Lord, we give you the praise. We give you the honor, and we give you the glory. This is a day that we haven't seen before. This is a situation we haven't gone through before, but Lord we believe your Word when you said you'll never leave us, nor forsake us, we believe you, Lord. We believe you!"

It was like a prayer watch meeting, when you specifically go to church only to pray. The time hadn't mattered, nor did the other appointments. God came into the room for a reason. Strength was needed and wanted, and sure enough, given. Guidance was the way, the Lord was having His way.

The prayers immediately touched Mrs. Gregory, and they gave her the extra edge to release her warm spiritual feeling. She spoke in tongues and it echoed throughout the moderate office. They all praised God in their own individual ways. Glory was amongst them all. With prayers going up, blessings were sure to come down. That's where Gracie took over.

"I just want to thank you," she said. "I just want to thank you in advance, Lord. You've given me strength where I knew my spirit was weak. I can only ask for your will to be done in my life. I pray that I continue to live as you want me to live. It's in your hands. I trust in you and lean on you. No other do I know. I thank you for the relationship I'm allowed to have with you. These and other blessings I ask in your name, Lord. Thank God, Amen!"

Mr. Gregory had to turn and face the door because his praises had not yet subsided. Gracie stood and joined her father in a hug. She loved to see her father praise the Lord. That let her know that real men could praise God!

There wasn't a dry eye in the office as Sandy picked up a slender envelope from her desk.

"Gracie, do you want to read them and let us know?"

she asked. "I haven't looked over the results yet. I felt it would be your right to know before anyone else."

"I'm okay," Gracie replied. She took in a cleansing breath and nodded. "You can go ahead."

Sandy tried to be professional and stoic, but her hands shook as she opened the envelope and removed the document. Gracie never watched anyone as intently as she watched Sandy and the blank expression on her face.

Sandy looked up from the paper and over to Grace and her parents.

"Gracie," she said in a voice thick with emotion, "your HIV status is negative." A few tears escaped from her eyes.

In slow motion, all the tension inside of Gracie built into the very center of her being. She looked at her mother who was nodding. Her father's eyes were closed, and he was whispering, "Thank you, God."

The tension continued to build and grow until Gracie asked, "It's negative?" and reached for the results. In red, Gracie read the word NEGATIVE in small letters. She raised her face to heaven and the tension rushed from her body, out into the atmosphere. "Only by the grace of God!" she yelled, tears streaming down her face.

The hard part was over. The scare wasn't.

As she ended the meeting, Sandy explained how even though the first initial test wasn't positive, Gracie would have to be tested several other times, regularly, over the next year because she had been in contact with someone who was positive. It was best to abstain from sex so that unseen antibodies couldn't be transmitted to a partner in case a later test proved that she was positive.

That was the least of Gracie's worries now. Sex had gotten her into this situation in the first place. In the future, her boyfriend, fiancé—whatever "he" wanted to be called—wasn't going to risk her life at all. She made a vow to the Lord to keep on His path and not that of her own. Because of that, things in her life was surely going to change. She made her appointments for HIV testing, and promised to get tested annually.

On the ride home with her parents, Gracie felt that she could start over, but thought about the two people who had tried their best, unsuccessfully, to hunt her down. Since Kendra had gone to Sean's hometown for the holidays, she didn't want to burden her friend with her problems. But as soon as Kendra returned, Gracie would just have to make the call and accept the yells. For Marcus, Gracie had no idea where to start. The whole story that lay before her was still sensitive to explain.

At home with her parents and thankful for her negative results, Gracie rested in her room and searched for all the energy she had lost in the past day's events. Later that night, after she had gotten rest and strength to feel like herself again, Gracie sat in the front room with her parents and cried. She felt blessed and could hardly believe that she was only one smart move away from being a statistic in the deadly world of AIDS. Again, with her parents' comfort, they let her know that she was special and that it was God's grace that had kept her. Gracie thanked God.

She was still debating on phoning her best friend. Gracie stayed busy on her laptop while her father watched football, half asleep, and her mother put the finishing touches on the cake she had baked for Christmas.

Gracie was searching, but she didn't know what she

was searching for. She had so many ideas about what she wanted to do with her HIV scare. Her ideas would now make her an activist for HIV and AIDS, and she was proud of that. She had a testimony that would help save others.

While surfing the internet, Gracie came across the website of a woman, living in Dallas. She was in her mid-thirties and had been living with HIV for seven years. Gracie read its entirety. She found it a blessing on the woman's behalf that the woman was able to cope through faith, even though she now had AIDS. The woman on the website wasn't giving up. When Gracie read of the woman's dedication to teach young men and women about the risks of unprotected sex, she decided that she would make an appointment with the lady and help her help others. Without hesitation, Gracie sent an e-mail to the lady.

She got up from the comfortable position she had been in for the past couple of hours. She went into the bathroom to run her bath water before bed. Sitting on the toilet, Gracie tried to decide if she should get in contact with Dillian or not. When her mother knocked on the door, Gracie ushered her in, but couldn't hide her full eyes fast enough.

"Honey, you alright?"

Forgetting about hiding her tears, Gracie looked up at her mother with a full heart. "I don't think so. I guess I'll be this way for a while, crying and all. It's just that . . ." Knowing that Dillian was the culprit, Gracie found it hard to tell her mother about the message that Dillian had left. "Dillian left a message on my machine the other day. He has HIV."

"It's okay . . . it's okay." Not drastically surprised about the news, Mrs. Gregory opened her arms to Gracie. "Gracie, I know that is a hard pill to swallow. It is for me. Just thank God that he finally called you. Be strong, honey."

There were no comforting words, no lullabies from her mother that would soothe her, no relaxing position. All Gracie wanted to do was soak in hot water and rest . . . and she did.

With her journal in tow, Gracie retreated from the bathroom and into her bedroom. She sat in the middle of her bed. Making a point to let herself heal through words, Gracie jotted her thoughts.

Today was another blessed day. I got a second chance at life. I got a second chance to clean up my act, STAY closer to God, and help bring others closer. With my second chance, I plan on doing more, loving more, caring more and help others care for themselves more, all in the love for Jesus. I'm simply blessed through God.

She wanted to save the rest for her testimony for others. As soon as she thought about the others she needed to talk to, Gracie immediately thought about Marcus and Kendra.

Gracie had never kept a secret from Kendra before and only did so this time because it wasn't something that people could easily share. She planned on sitting her friend down after Christmas and letting her know why she had become distant. Gracie really wanted to get it over with, but she dared not ruin her best friend's holiday.

The same with Marcus. Gracie really cared about Marcus. She always had and always would. She didn't know exactly what to say to him, but she would just have to take her chances on whether he would understand.

He had always been understanding. But this was a deadly disease that would still be a conversational piece for years. Gracie didn't know how understanding he would be. She wished she had done things differently in terms of dodging calls and so forth, but she didn't ride herself too hard. Gracie knew that no one could actually say what they would and wouldn't do in such situations. All she could pray for was that he would forgive her for cutting him off. She hoped Marcus would allow her back into his life.

CHAPTER TWENTY-SIX

Gracie woke up early on Christmas morning. She wanted to surprise her parents with breakfast in bed, but her plan was pushed to the side when she walked into her living room and saw a real Christmas tree, fully decorated. Her parents obviously wanted to make sure Gracie's Christmas was Christmas.

She had a full grin on her face the entire time she was preparing breakfast. Gracie knew that she was special and that her parents thought so as well. She thought of the times when she would worry in secret because she thought she would upset her parents. Gracie was proud to know that her parents were there for her through it all. They had showed her that she could always lean on them.

Gracie knocked on the guest bedroom door and very slowly proceeded to open it to find her parents waking. She smiled and moved toward them carefully, placing their breakfast tray on the bed.

"Merry Christmas," she whispered. "It's not too early is it?"

Gracie nestled herself at the bottom of the queen-sized sleigh bed and gave them small pats on their legs.

"What time is it?" Gracie's father asked, rubbing at his eyes.

"It's seven o'clock," Gracie chided. "Don't tell me you're still sleepy."

"Aw, he ain't sleepy," Gracie's mother said. She picked a strawberry from the small dish of cut fruit. "Just old. I made him stay up with me to decorate the tree. Oooh, I hope I didn't spoil that for you."

"Don't worry about it, Momma. I already saw the tree, and it's absolutely wonderful. Y'all are just too sweet to me."

Gracie leapt up from the bed and hustled over to her mother's side of the bed to give her a big hug. She did the same to her father.

"Eat up," she said, walking to the door. "I'll see you guys in a bit."

Gracie went into her bedroom. Immediately, she picked up her Bible to read her daily scripture. When she read the scripture in Matthew about forgiving the sins of your brother, Gracie thought of Dillian and knew she had unfinished business. She sat the Bible on her lap and picked up the cordless phone from the nightstand and dialed.

When she told her parents her plans for the morning, Gracie practically had to beg them to let her talk to Dillian alone. She finally got them to understand that this was between her and her ex-fiancé. She needed to close this chapter of her life alone. Gracie dialed Dillian's room number, determined to see him.

"I'm coming up there Dillian," Gracie announced as

soon as Dillian answered his hospital's line. Gracie spoke once again. "Did you hear me?"

"I hear you Gracie, but it really isn't necessary. I . . ."

"What *do* you mean? Dillian, I need to know why you didn't you tell me. I need to know—I need to see you. I need to do this for myself."

"I don't want you to see me like this," Dillian responded as he looked at himself.

"Dillian, I'm not even worried about that. You owe me this!" Gracie became aggravated at the thought of Dillian turning her away.

Knowing Gracie wasn't going to take no for an answer, Dillian obliged. "Well, you know where I'm at. I'll be here. It'll be good to see you, Gracie." He was hoping for a similar response. He returned the receiver to its cradle as the dial-tone sounded.

Dillian's door was cracked open. Gracie stood in it counting to ten before walking in. The room was bright and white and housed only Dillian. Before this moment, Gracie had tried hard to imagine what Dillian would look like or if he would have tubes running every which way. When she walked in and saw him lying peacefully on his side, her nervousness lessened.

"Dillian?" she whispered as she stepped closer. "Are you asleep?"

Turning to face someone he thought he could never face again took a lot of energy for Dillian. Though his physical appearance hadn't changed drastically in the last few months, his motions told his story. He had spent so much energy running from his problems and beating himself up over what had happened. He cursed himself time and time again for the mistakes that he had made in the past, both known and unknown to Gracie.

"Hey, I'm up," he said. "Come on in."

He motioned for Gracie to come closer. He had hoped she wouldn't be afraid. By the looks of her, Gracie was far from scared.

With unexpected tears in her eyes, Gracie sat her purse in an empty chair and went to sit on the bed with Dillian. Gracie leaned in to give him a hug. In her gut, two emotions were battling one another. She was angry and sad. Beyond all the hurt, she could not completely turn away from Dillian. All the things she thought would come out of her mouth wouldn't even reach the surface.

"Oh, Dillian," Gracie said, digging her forehead into his shoulder. "Why didn't you tell me?"

Dillian pulled Gracie up and looked into her eyes, something he hadn't been able to do ever since he'd gotten his results earlier in the year.

"Gracie, I don't know," he answered. "I found out when you kept telling me to go to the doctor at the beginning of the year. When I *did* find out, I couldn't tell you. I was too ashamed. The thought of you being infected didn't make it any better for me either. Thank God you're not."

Dillian had made Gracie tell him the news of her negative results over the phone. He needed to hear her tell him before he felt he could do anything else. When he heard the results through the phone, he was grateful to God for sparing Gracie's life, even though he hadn't been so lucky himself.

"So all this time," Gracie was fighting tears, "all this time, you were talking about a knee injury and that wasn't the real story, was it?" Gracie wiped her tears from her face with the back of her hand. After all that she had gone through in just a week's time, she could only imagine how Dillian had been suffering with his diagnosis all alone.

Dillian nodded.

She closed her eyes, attempting to calm the tide of questions that splashed through her mind. Not one subsided, and she released what she had tried to keep in.

"How did you get it, Dillian?" she asked. "How long have you had it?"

After Dillian explained his steroid use and contact with a bad batch, the room became silent. Gracie was speechless. In a weird way, Gracie was thankful that she didn't have to hear about Dillian sleeping around on her and coming in contact with the virus that way. Nevertheless, contracting the disease itself was bad enough, no matter how he had gotten it.

Dillian's nurse came in to administer his meds, breaking the stale silence. "Good afternoon Mr. McNab . . . oh, hello there," she said to Gracie. "I'm sorry to intrude, but Mr. McNab, you need to take your medication."

"Will I need to leave?" Gracie asked the nurse. She was looking directly at Dillian as he turned to his side, exposing his hip for the coming shot.

"Nonsense, you stay seated. He's getting the hang of things now . . . isn't that right Mr. Universe?" Dillian's nurse asked. She already had given him his first round of meds.

"Oh, yeah," Dillian answered, keeping his sight off both women.

"Hopefully you can be a source of continual support for our good patient," the young, swift nurse suggested to Gracie. "I'm really happy that you've started participating in your recovery." Seeing Dillian's arched eyebrows, she continued, "Yes your 'recovery'."

Gracie was listening to the nurse more than Dillian was. She asked him about the nurse's directions for his medication intake and taking care of himself, after she'd exited the room.

"Dillian, what is she talking about, take your medicine and eat your meals? Are you not doing what you're supposed to do?"

"Well, that's the reason I'm in here to begin with," Dillian answered. "I can't go out like this, Gracie. I can't take twenty-some-odd different medications everyday for the rest of my life . . . however long that will be."

"But you have to. It's for your own good. You can't just give up. I mean honestly, what sense does that make? You said you took steroids and took them on a daily basis just about. Now, for your own well being, you can't take the medicines that will save your life? You have to, Dillian."

"Why not? Why can't I give up? What kind of life can I have? Let's face it: you're not going to marry me or have kids with me. I won't have a family, and I don't want to be alone."

"So you're just going to give up on life because your life has taken you down a different road? Dillian, when I found out that I might be infected, I lost it. I threw things, broke things, and even thought about taking my own life. But for what? Just because I wouldn't have the ideal life any longer?

"When I realized that God thought enough about me to bring me into this world, no matter what, I couldn't let Him down, so I slowly accepted it. Heck, what else could I do? I realized I had family that loved me, and all and all, I loved myself. You're right though. I won't sit up here and pretend with you that I will take up where we left off, but I want you to know that I'm your friend until I can't be your friend any longer. And that's not even possible."

Dillian could not stop crying. He couldn't believe it. Outside of his family, Gracie was the only person he needed support from. He shook his head, unable to believe Gracie's devoted friendship.

"How can you do this, Gracie?" he asked. "I have hurt you so much. I could have destroyed your life!"

Gracie remained strong though the tears welled up. She pulled Dillian to her and hugged him.

"All is forgiven Dillian," she said. "I can't hold anything against you. True, I may cry every time I think about it, or when I look at you, but what would I gain for turning my back on you? I love you."

The two held onto each other and cried, not questioning the past or the future. They sat for another hour talking about the level of their friendship. Dillian still had undying love for Gracie and he knew that he would have to pray for extra strength and comfort. She told him that her parents were in the waiting room and wanted to see him. They waited because of her decision to see him alone. He requested their presence.

For the most part, his Christmas was okay. As well as it could be, anyway. He found hope deep down inside. With the prayers from Gracie and her family, he chose to give his now complicated life another chance. He planned on doing everything possible to ensure he was around until God told him it was over.

Even though he felt better and considered life more precious, there was still something more he had to tell Gracie. He promised himself he would tell her and soon. He just hoped that she could stand strong through it all.

Gracie felt peace all through her being as she drove her parents back to her apartment to start on the

Christmas turkey. She felt fresh and new. She looked around as she drove silently, praying about her second chance to live life freely. As they pulled up to her condo complex, Gracie saw Marcus's car. He must have gotten her voicemail saying that she was ready to talk.

"Well, looky here," Gracie's father said as he saw Marcus. "What's going on, man?"

"Aw, nothing, Mr. Gregory," Marcus responded. He stared at Gracie. "Just coming by to chat with Gracie, I hope."

"Okay, well, we'll leave you two alone." Gracie's father grabbed his wife's hand and pulled her into the apartment. "Come on, old woman, let's go into the house and leave these kids alone."

"Not until I get me a kiss from this handsome man." Gracie's mother waltzed up to Marcus and planted a kiss on his cheek.

Gracie and Marcus watched as her parents went inside. They stood in silence, staring at the apartment.

"Want to go for a ride?" Gracie asked.

"Who's driving?" Marcus replied. "Me or you?" He pointed between the two with his index finger.

"You—since you asked."

"Sure thing."

Marcus reached his hand out. Gracie lowered her head but met Marcus's hand with one of her own. He brought it to his mouth and kissed it gently.

Gracie hoped he would still feel the same way after he found out her reason for disappearing. A few moments later, Marcus and Gracie sat out front of a small café, sipping mochas.

"You surprised me," Gracie said after awhile. "Seeing you at my apartment when we pulled up . . ."

"Well, you surprised me when you left the message,"

he retorted. "Especially since you haven't been answering or returning my phone calls all week."

"Believe me, it was a long week, Marcus."

"Tell me about it. I'm listening."

Taking a sip of her drink before she started, Gracie knew it was all or nothing.

"The day that you called, asking me those questions, Marcus . . . I knew what you were talking about. I was afraid."

"So there is a certain reason why Dillian left you?"

"Yes . . . Dillian is HIV positive." Starring down at her cup, Gracie breathed in a steady breath and waited for Marcus's reaction. There wasn't one.

Several minutes passed by before either said a word. Gracie was waiting for Marcus to etch in.

"So, it was true? What about you, Gracie? Is that why you cut me off? Are you infected as well?"

"I'm not. I've been tested and I'm not. Granted, I do have other tests to take, but I protected myself. I'm sorry, Marcus, but this was and still is all too scary."

Pouring out her entire episode, Gracie had just about finished her mocha while Marcus was still holding a full cup. Too engrossed in Gracie's story to drink, he just listened.

"I figured it had to be that. I hate to say it, but Michelle was the one giving me the leads to what was going on in your life. I wish it had been you."

"Michelle? Hmm. I can only imagine what her motive was. I'll worry about that later. But, Marcus I was too afraid. I'm sorry, but if my results had been different, there was no way I could have faced you."

"And to be honest, if they would have been different, I don't know what would have happened either. But one thing is for sure; I would still be here for you. Did you think different?"

"Of course I thought different. I'm not dumb to the fact that this virus breaks up friendships, marriages, and families. But you know it's not over for me. What if things change? What if my second test results reveal that I'm positive?"

"We'll have to cross that road when we get there. I know that being with you is all that I'm looking for right now, and hopefully you feel the same way."

"I do, but—"

"But . . . just let it happen. Whatever it is we need to do, let's do it. I just want to do it together. I lost you once, but I don't plan on losing you again in this lifetime. Remember, we've been down the physical road. This gives us an opportunity to learn more about one another."

Marcus's words were music to Gracie's ears. She was afraid to believe, but she didn't want to doubt it. Again she was going to let go and let God. If it were too good to be true, only time would tell. But the feeling that she had in her heart said that the adventure with Marcus was indeed good and true.

Gracie had officially made this Christmas the best Christmas of all. After finishing up their mochas, Marcus asked Gracie if she'd like to go by his house for a while. She agreed.

Driving down Marcus's street was slow going. It seemed as if every house on the street had planned to have their Christmas parties that night. As they pulled up to the curb in front of Marcus's house, Gracie asked what he knew she was going to ask.

"Whose cars are those in your driveway, Marcus?"

He took the key out of the car's ignition. He turned to look at Gracie and only smiled. Smiling back, she continued to ask the same question until they were on the porch, about to enter.

His family. The mood at Marcus's house had Gracie fighting back tears. She had no idea that his family had come into town to visit with him, but she didn't regret being in the midst of the small family's holiday. Fitting in like old times, she sat around his mother, step-father, sister, and brother, and the rest of the family. Gracie always felt at home with them.

She moved through the house playing games, watched Christmas specials on TV, and ate some of the best food she had ever tasted. Gracie hoped that the feeling she had around Marcus was mutual and that it would last a good while.

She ensured that she stayed long enough, but not too long. Gracie let Marcus know when it was time to get back to her parents. She gave out hugs and kisses and promised that she'd start visiting again. Gracie and Marcus headed to the other side of town.

When they made it back to her address, Gracie wouldn't let Marcus leave without eating a few bites with her and her parents as well. Luckily for him, there was room on the sofas to sprawl out. After they ate, they were all too tired to move.

After the first movie, during which they drank hot chocolate, Marcus leaned over and kissed Gracie on the forehead. He told her it was getting late and he had to leave.

Walking him to the door was just like back in the day. They fit so well. It was proven indeed that, "if it is love, let it go, and if it comes back, it was meant to be." Love had come back home.

CHAPTER TWENTY-SEVEN

The rest of the week, things slowly returned to normal for Gracie. By Friday, she was back in the swing of things. Anticipating Kendra's call to let her know she had made it back from the big east, Gracie dialed Kendra's number to leave a message.

"Kendra! Heffa, you at home and didn't call me?"

"Hey, girl. I've been home. We had to leave and come back the day after Christmas; I'm sicker than a dog."

"Well stay put. I'm coming over. You need me to bring you anything?"

"Just yourself. I have a slight fever, so Sean brought me some soup on his lunch break."

"Alrighty. Well, let me ask you, are you up for talking?"

"Of course! I'm just happy you finally came out of your funk. Bring yourself, girl."

And that's what Gracie planned on doing. Running around her bed and into her closet to find her favorite jogging suit, Gracie changed out of her lounging shorts. She heard her cell phone ring and dropped her tennis shoes as she went to her dresser where her phone sat.

"Hello, Gracie?"

"Yes. Hi, Dillian. Is everything okay?" She wasn't expecting Dillian's phone call.

"Uh, yeah. I was just calling you. Are you busy right now? . . . I really need to talk to you."

"Actually, I'm on my way over to Kendra's. How about I give you a call a little later?"

Dillian obliged and decided to just wait, especially once he heard of Gracie's plans.

"It can wait. That'll be fine. Gracie . . . call me, I really need to talk to you, okay?"

"Alright I will."

Gracie didn't expect to see her and the apartment in such disarray. Kendra's hair was uncombed, the place wasn't clean, and loose papers were all over the place.

"Dang, Kendra," Gracie said with a pout on her face. "I would hug you, but I don't want the flu."

"Girl, I know. Ain't it a mess? I'm happy you're feeling better. Want something to drink?"

"Hot tea if you got it."

"One hot tea coming up."

Kendra walked into the kitchen to put on a kettle of water. She was happy to see that whatever was holding Gracie in darkness had been lifted. Fiddling with her pots and pans, Kendra hurried to get her kettle situated so she could give Gracie her undivided attention. She walked back into the living room.

"So, what's the deal, friend?" Kendra asked.

Gracie patted the empty spot on the sofa right next to her. Kendra sat beside her and gave a light tap to one of Gracie's knees.

"It seems like a lifetime," Gracie began, "but for the last past week, I've been through the storm."

"Why?" Kendra asked. She took in Gracie's serious disposition and grew frightened. "What is it, Gracie? You're scaring me."

"I'm sorry, I don't mean to scare you, but it was all so scary for me." Gracie searched for strength to tell this story just one more time.

"I found out why Dillian left me," Gracie said. "He's sick."

"He's sick? Did you see him somewhere or something? What do you mean, sick?"

"No." Gracie stilled herself before she finished with, "Kendra, Dillian has HIV."

"What?"

Kendra's shock blended with the teakettle's screams. Kendra's eyes bounced around the room, trying to figure out where the screams were coming from. Tears sprung to her eyes, but she managed to get up and stumble into the kitchen to take the kettle off of the stove's burner.

"Oh no," Kendra cried as she turned off the stove and picked up the kettle. Too distraught to pay attention, Kendra placed her free hand on the bottom of the kettle. Heat shot through her hand and she yelled out, yelled out for the pain in her hand and from Gracie's devastating news.

Gracie heard Kendra's screams and came barreling into the kitchen. She figured Kendra was torn up over the news and felt horrible for her and Dillian. Gracie threw her arms around Kendra.

"Ken! Kendra! It's okay. I'm in the clear. I tested negative. Thanks to God I used protection." When Gracie saw that that didn't calm Kendra, she was confused.

"Kendra?" Gracie asked.

Gracie released Kendra. Kendra turned to face her with a silent worried, blank look on her face. Kendra trembled, and Gracie pulled her close.

"Oh my goodness, Gracie!" Kendra's eyes were so wide, they could have fallen from their sockets. "I never thought it would be something like that! How do you know? How did you find out?" Kendra asked as she tried to steady her body.

"I got a call from the health department. Dillian turned my name in."

Kendra gripped Gracie's arm. Her grip made Gracie wince.

"Kendra," she said, looking down at her friend's hold. "It's okay. I'm fine, sis."

"How long has he been carrying the virus, Gracie?" Kendra asked in a voice as quiet and soft as air.

Gracie looked away for a moment, her eyes fluttering. She fought to keep the tears in.

"The doctors say for almost two years now."

Gracie let out a short cry when Kendra went limp in her arms. Gracie wrapped her arms around Kendra's middle tightly.

"Kendra! Are you okay?"

"No," Kendra replied. A loud sob escaped between her lips. "No, no, no! I don't think I am okay. I'm sorry, Gracie."

Kendra fell back against a picture frame in the hallway and slid down to the floor in an emotional heap.

"Kendra, it's going to be all right," Gracie said, stunned at Kendra's reaction. "I've even talked to Dillian and he's pulling through."

Kendra shook her head no. "It's not going to be all right," she whispered. "It makes total sense now," she said with a slur.

Kendra looked up, and through her watery eyes, she saw Gracie's confusion.

"What are you talking about, Kendra?"

Kendra placed her cold, clammy hands over her face. When she removed them, she saw Gracie sliding down the opposite wall facing her. Kendra took small breaths between her cries.

"Gracie," she said through her tears, "if Dillian has HIV and he contracted it almost two years ago, them more than likely... that's . . . that's where I contracted the virus."

Neither spoke for several moments. Gracie was the first to break the confused silence.

"What?" Gracie asked somberly. She threw her hands out to implore Kendra to explain. "I don't get it. Just because Dillian has it, you feel you have it? Wh— What's going on?"

Kendra turned her head and coughed.

She was getting angry, but she didn't want to jump the gun. Gracie wanted to be sure. "Speak, Kendra. Tell me what you're talking about."

"I have HIV, Gracie." Kendra moaned. "I planned on telling you. Just not like this." She started rumbling. "When you started asking about me and Sean . . . my going out. I didn't know how to." Kendra's guilt spilled out and she started rambling. "You don't care. You never listen, Gracie. You have no idea what I went through as a child. He raped me. He raped me for almost three years!" Kendra rambled as tears covered her wearied face. "My momma didn't want me. She don't want me," Kendra looked up with tears in her eyes. "My uncle raped me, Gracie."

"Ken?" When Kendra didn't respond, Gracie crawled over to her and shook her. "Kendra. What is going on? Where are you getting at? You're HIV positive?"

"My doctor. Ha! He told me and I was going to tell you. I was going to tell Sean. But drinking was easier. Then the wreck, and then I couldn't. I was scared. I'm scared, Gracie!" Kendra said, turning the conversation into a counseling session.

Kendra's head slowly rolled back against the wall, and she stared Gracie.

As her friend shook her with all her energy, Kendra snapped out of her trance.

"Gracie, I slept with Dillian."

On her drive home, Gracie drove slow to keep her car on the road. She couldn't stop crying. The pain had just shattered her already damaged heart. In all her most horrific nightmares, she never expected anything like this. Not her best friend. Not Kendra. Not Dillian.

No one could have gotten her ready to believe this soap opera of a nightmare. First her fiancé was a carrier of a deadly virus, and now her best friend was in the middle of it all.

She had already called Marcus and asked him to meet her at her apartment, but there was another call she needed to make. Thinking back to the conversation, it now made sense why Dillian seemed nervous but persistent for her to call. Is that what he wanted to talk about?

At a stoplight, Gracie took out her cell phone and dialed.

"Hello, Dillian's room?" His mother answered.

"Uh, Mrs. McNab, this is Gracie. May I speak to Dillian?"

"Sure, honey. Give me one moment," she replied, handing Dillian the phone.

"Hello?"

Those two syllables ripped Gracie's heart apart and she bawled.

"Gracie," Dillian said, "I'm so sorry! It was a mistake. I made a big mistake. I wanted to tell you."

"How could you?" Gracie screamed into the phone. She jumped when the car behind her blew its horn. The light was green. She tapped the gas and moved forward. "Not only did you leave me, but you took my best friend with you!"

Silence gripped the phone.

"You don't have anything to say?" Gracie demanded. "It was a mistake, is all you can come up with? Dillian, how could you sleep with my best friend? I trusted you and this is what you give me. As if almost infecting me wasn't enough! You made sure I was left with nothing or no one, right? I said, 'right'?"

Gracie took three short breaths.

"Look," she said as calmly as she could. "I'm gong to let you go. I've bitten off more than I can swallow. Oh, and by the way, I don't care to ever hear from you again. You, your family . . . everything having to do with you is null and void."

Gracie threw her cell phone to the floor on the passenger's side without pushing the end button. She just wanted to get home, into Marcus's arms.

"Dillian and Kendra," Gracie uttered before letting out a wounded cry.

When she had heard the words come out of Kendra's mouth, her first mind told her to slap the words right back in. Instead, she grabbed her and shook. But no matter how long or how hard she shook her friend, she wouldn't take it back.

After the crying and begging, Gracie didn't know what she was asking for. Gracie sat inches away from

Kendra and demanded her now ex-friend, tell her why, when, and where she betrayed her.

"Gracie, please don't do this! I made a mistake. Blame it on me, but just don't go there," Kendra pleaded.

Kendra tried to get up, but Gracie forcefully pushed her back against the wall. She couldn't help but see Kendra differently at that moment. Everything came together. The guys that she trained, men who came up to her in the mall, the guy she had sexed in their office. It was now all clear.

In college, she had been the only one who didn't see it. Gracie was the only female friend that Kendra had. Other girls tried to warn her, but she just thought that they were mistaken. Once, Erica, a dorm mate tried to come to Gracie's rescue.

"Gracie, how can you be in such denial, girl? That girl is just going to keep burning you!" Erica raised her angry voice at Gracie.

"Erica, please. You gotsta be kidding if you think that Ian and Kendra are having sex. That's not the reason why he ain't returning my calls. I guess he's studying hard for finals."

". . . Or studying hard up on ya girl, Kendra. I saw them with my own eyes, soror."

"Well, here she comes now. Let me just ask her." Waiting for her roommate to come closer, Gracie dove in once she was in ear shot.

"Say, Kendra! Erica said she saw you and Ian getting down." She looked back at Erica and continued. "I told her that it couldn't be you because you're my home-girl."

When Gracie looked at her friend, she saw the fear, hurt, and pain in her face that said it all. Gracie ran past Kendra and out of the dormitory.

From that moment on, she fed Kendra with a long

handle spoon, but Gracie forgave her when Kendra explained.

Now as her strength started to leave her again, Gracie demanded Kendra's response.

"You owe me that much!" Gracie yelled. "Kendra, you slept with my boyfriend! My fiancé! Do you not think you owe me a reason? I want to know and I want to know now!"

"I know I do, alright! I owe you!"

Kendra tried to catch her breath so that she could talk, but it was futile.

After waiting what seemed like forever, Gracie hissed, "I'm waiting! Your crying now doesn't even compare, Kendra. It doesn't compare to what I've been through this week. I thought it was just Dillian, but you've put me through hell too! And don't try to put this on me, Kendra."

Standing, Kendra headed for the living room. "Let's go in here."

When Gracie grabbed her by the arm, Kendra was forced to halt.

"Just tell me. I'm not up for the college replay. We are now in the real world, *sista,* and you've stabbed me in my back again!" She was getting angrier by the minute. "I must be a fool! Thinking that all those men were just friends! Kendra, what are you? Are you a . . ."

Falling back against the wall, Kendra screamed, "It happened about a year and a half ago, okay!"

"In the first months of our relationship?"

"About six months after. It was when me and Sean were on bad terms. I, we, didn't plan on it."

"Like I'm supposed to believe anything you say. Just tell me . . . I'm listening."

"It was around the time you went to the photo shoot in Washington."

"For the fitness magazine?"

"Yeah. It just happened. He came up to the gym around closing time and . . ."

"In my gym, Kendra? My place? Kendra, you're telling me that you had an affair with *my* fiancé in *my* place of business. My sweat and tears?"

Gracie slapped Kendra hard and solid across the face. Gracie rushed past her delusional peer out of the apartment. Outside, she bent over and vomited. She wondered when this real-life nightmare would be over. Just when she thought she'd survived, more horrible secrets were revealed.

Gracie lost all of her energy when she saw Marcus waiting for her outside of her apartment. She fell into his arms, and her tears soaked his shoulder.

After he listened to her cry and yell like her soul was being ripped from her body, Marcus turned her to him.

"Are you finished?" he asked.

"What do you mean?" she sniffled.

"I just want to know if you're finished. I mean if you're not, honey, cry until you have it out of your system."

"I have no choice but to be done actually," Gracie said, wiping tears from her face.

"Now listen." Marcus stroked Gracie's cheek. "It's over. Everything is out in the open. I know you feel as though you have been betrayed, and I can see why. It all seems surreal to the point that I wouldn't believe it if I didn't know you."

He held both of her hands close to his heart. He wanted Gracie to feel his true love. "What I'm trying to say, Gracie, is because I see your pain, I can't help but hurt with you. That's how I know I'm going to be here for you. I want to give my all to keep you from going through anymore pain. If you allow me, I will. I'll be here."

Marcus went to gather a throw to cover her. Gracie sat in awe at how her world had been turned upside down in a matter of months. She didn't know how it was possible. Before she could wallow in it alone, Marcus was there to help her through the embarrassing, unbelievable trials.

Marcus made sure that Gracie was comfortable for bed. He was about to kiss her goodnight and good-bye, but Gracie hugged him and asked him to stay until she fell asleep. Deep in her soul, she knew she would make it and be all right, but she knew that this night wasn't the time.

Marcus wanted nothing more than to stay and comfort her. All he could think about was their chance meeting. He knew that God had a hand in it. Marcus didn't question God, he just knew that this was where God wanted him, and that was fine with him.

CHAPTER TWENTY-EIGHT

After Dillian hung up the phone, he knew that the end had come. He had decided to tell her about Kendra, but Kendra had beaten him to the punch.

As he lay in the bed, Dillian went through scenario after scenerio about how the conversation went. He hadn't quite decided how he would have told Gracie. He just knew it had to be done. Dillian did know that he couldn't tell her over the phone, but he knew it wouldn't be easy to tell her to her face either.

As Dillian wondered how Kendra felt about it, he decided to call her. He had to. Not calling wouldn't be right at all.

Leaning over, Dillian picked up the receiver of the phone. He pressed the '0' button before lying back in bed.

"Operator. How can I help you?"

"Yes, can I please get the residential listing for Kendra Jackson?"

"Please hold for the number."

*The number is 214-555-5555. Press "1" to be con-
nected to your call.*

Dillian pressed "1". He wondered if Kendra would
even talk to him. He didn't know how, but he knew he
had to get her to accept his apology and understand
that he had no idea that he was infected.

As soon as the phone began to ring, Dillian thought
about the possibility of Sean answering the line. Just
when he was about to put the receiver back on the hook,
he heard a woman's voice.

"Gracie . . . is that you?" Kendra asked.

"This is . . . Dillian." Silence. "I know you probably
can't gain the strength to talk to me at this moment,
and it's perfectly all right if you can't, but if you can
just listen, I'd like to say that I'm sorry." Tears choked
him. "Now I know that isn't much, but . . ."

"It's okay," Kendra finally answered in a monotone.

"What was that?" Dillian asked in fast whisper.

"It's okay, Dillian. I already knew I was infected.
The only question I had was where I had contracted it
from. That was the only shocking news of the day. Actually, when Gracie came over, I had planned on
telling her about my status. Other than that, I had no
idea. But don't feel bad for me at all. It's not about me.
I feel bad for Gracie."

Not really knowing which direction to go in, Dillian
started in. "I feel the same. But I need you to know
that I feel bad for what I've done to you as well," Dillian waited for a response, but then continued. "So you
already knew you had it? I don't know what to say.
Why didn't you contact me?"

"For what? You should know how hard it is to come
to terms with all of this anyway. Nothing about this is
easy." It was easier for her to say that, instead of let-

ting the truth be known that she had no idea from whom she had contracted it. Her black book was so thick and she had such frequent contact with men that she couldn't even put faces with names at times.

"Right. I understand. I guess I should be grateful that you understand the whole situation. I feel so weird. If I could take it all back, I want you to know that I would."

Nonchalantly, Kendra responded, "Sure. But that's just not how it works, so I don't even play that game with myself. All this time I . . . I had been going through . . . knowing that I had slept with you and possibly infected you . . . it's been rough, which in turn could have infected Gracie. You have no idea what I've been going through, maybe with the sickness, but not the mental damage. Then just knowing that the truth would have to come out made it no better."

Silence.

"Everything is such a blur now," Kendra mumbled. "This one alone has put the icing on my withered cake. It just goes to show you, to live is to die and to die is to gain. But what should I gain? I'm not worth anything. No good.

"I've shattered so many lives in so many ways, just because of what I thought I needed. Thinking that I could just sleep with my best friend's fiancé and suffer no consequences. Well, I've proven God wrong. I can make a mess of the life He's given me. I'm nothing." Kendra sat and cried.

Dillian responded. "I understand, Kendra. I feel the same way. I feel as if there is nothing left. I've taken my life, your life, and I've taken a part of Gracie away. You're not the only one who has to suffer conse-quences. I'm sure I'll have to suffer more since I'm the ring leader."

They sat on the phone and cried. Not because of what happened, they had already cried over that. They cried because something they had done in lust for quick satisfaction now left them feeling less than human.

For several hours, Dillian and Kendra cried, talked, and cried some more. They finally settled into a somber conversation about the one thing that they had learned plenty about: HIV.

Kendra went on to explain to him what led her to the doctor's office. She had battled what she figured was sinuses and allergies non-stop for several months. Kendra finally went to her physician and had them run a different test.

With the symptoms and the test results, Kendra's diagnosis turned out to be pneumonia. While she thought she had what many called "walking pneumonia," the physician explained that Kendra had Pneumocystis Carinii, a form of pneumonia that HIV patients usually contract. After the results from her blood work came back, Kendra found out that she indeed had been infected with the virus.

"Kendra, I'm sorry." Dillian couldn't stop feeling guilty, especially since it was all his fault.

"I told you, there's no need to keep apologizing. I got myself into this to begin with. There is only so much I can blame you for. And believe me, I've had my days. I've been through the emotional roller coaster and wanted to hate everyone. I'm doing better now, but it's still day-to day for me."

He appreciated Kendra's easiness about her situation. Dillian was blessed to have her understand that it takes two to tango even though he took full responsibility for their infection.

They talked more about being as healthy as they

could and compared medications and schedules. Dillian remembered that Kendra had a boyfriend and asked about him.

"So what did your boyfriend say?"

Kendra told Dillian that he had just broken up with her because of the lack of physical pleasure in their relationship. He felt sorry for her.

"Well, when I found out I had it, there was no doubt in my mind that I'd given it to Sean . . . my boyfriend. We never used protection, of course, because we trusted each other." She was disappointed that she hadn't told Sean. "He doesn't even know yet."

"Kendra! What are you waiting on? I know I'm not really the one to talk, but you have to let this man know. Look, When the time is right for you to let him know, I'll be that support you'll need to tell him, okay?"

Kendra let Dillian know that he could call her when he needed to talk to someone who really and truly understood. At that point, they vowed to be each other's crutch on the broken ground they would have to travel. Dillian even welcomed Kendra to the hospital's support group. Though she thanked him, Dillian knew Kendra was in the same mindset he had been in. She would accept the disease when the time was right for her.

CHAPTER TWENTY-NINE

Marcus knew that Gracie hated that he had to endure so much drama so early into their new
relationship. Little did she know that he was happy to
be around. He'd stepped up to the plate, and he didn't
mind giving his all. He knew that Gracie would do the
same for him. In so many ways, she already had. He
was proud that he was still around to help her through
it all, and even happier to help her bring in a blessed
New Year that she deserved.

When Gracie opened her door on New Year's Eve,
Marcus was there smiling with roses. Gracie flung
herself into his arms and hugged him so tight that he
wasn't sure she would ever let him go. He didn't want
her to.

"You never have to let go, you know," Marcus whispered into her ear.

"I know," Gracie said with a slight giggle, "but we'll
miss watch night service if I don't."

They laughed.

"I know," Marcus said, "but seriousl,. if you ever

think of putting up a guard against me, don't. I won't hurt you. Guaranteed."

Gracie's heart warmed to near boiling. She placed a small kiss on his lips and whispered, "Let's go."

The church service was awesome. The theme, "Out with the old, in with the new," was just the inspiration Gracie needed for her new year. She had her family's love, a man who adored her, and a Savior who did it all.

As she listened to the sermon, she decided that she was going to begin the New Year with a heart of forgiveness. She wasn't ready to see Dillian or Kendra yet, but she could forgive them. She knew she had the strength to do that, especially with God on her side.

The service progressed, and she and Marcus swayed to the music. Gracie didn't know if anyone else had a reason to shout and praise God. She did. As the crowded sanctuary counted down to the New Year, Gracie reached for the hills from whence she sought her help and praised the Lord for herself and for those who couldn't.

CHAPTER THIRTY

Gracie tried to begin her New Year as smoothly as possible. She promoted a few of her instructors to take over her workload while she spent more time running the business. She wasn't ready to face Kendra. However, Gracie's smooth life didn't last for long.

Two weeks into the New Year, she received a call from Kendra. They needed to meet and get their business in order. Gracie knew that the only way she could see Kendra was if Marcus went with her. She set up a meeting with all three of them.

God knew that Gracie needed to confront Kendra alone. The morning of the meeting, Marcus had to back out because of a last minute scouting run. Gracie paced and fought the urge to cancel the meeting.

As Gracie stepped through the front doors of her gym, she was instantly calmed. She couldn't believe that she had actually contemplated tearing the whole building down to make sure she would never be in the room that Kendra and Dillian had their affair. She fought the foolish spirit that wanted her to lose everything by facing it head on. Prayer indeed changed things for Gracie.

At the entrance to the office, Gracie sent a quick prayer into the air. Half of the office was bare. Kendra had packed up all her things and they were sitting beside the door. Across the office, Kendra sat quietly behind her desk. Gracie's anger changed into concern when she saw Kendra's face. Her face was colored black, blue, and red. The right side of her face was swollen from eye to chin.

"What in the world?" Gracie yelled before racing over to Kendra. "What happened to you, Kendra?"

Kendra raised her hands to ward Gracie off.

"Don't," she said, looking away.

"Who did this?" Gracie asked. She gently cupped Kendra's chin and turned her face back around. "Are you all right?"

Kendra sat back in her chair, trying to put space between herself and Gracie.

"I'll be all right," she said. "Sean."

"What?"

"You asked me who did it. Sean did it."

"Sean? Kendra, why?"

Gracie saw Kendra wince as tears leaked from her swollen eyes and tracked her bruised cheeks. She raced to her desk and grabbed a few tissues.

Kendra dabbed lightly at her tears. "Well, I waited until I thought it was okay to talk to him, and when I did, I had no choice but to tell him that I was positive so that he could get tested."

With a hung head, Gracie just reached across the desk and waited patiently for Kendra to reach back. As soon as their hands connected, Kendra told Gracie the entire story.

She told Gracie how she waited for Sean to arrive at her apartment during lunch to pick up the remainder of his things. That was when she presented him with her results. Sean read the results silently. When Kendra tried to apologize, he lashed out at her. With every word that came out of his mouth, he slapped, pushed, and eventually kicked her. He told her he was getting back at her for the virus he was sure that he had. He went to the closet and pulled out his 380 and held it to her temple. The only thing that halted his trigger finger were the knocks on the door.

"Everybody deals with it differently," Kendra concluded in a hushed voice. She shrugged and nodded her head as if she believed she deserved it.

"By almost killing someone?" Gracie shouted. "Kendra, he could have killed you. Did you go to the police?"

Mocking a laugh, Kendra continued. "I didn't have to. They came to us. I guess the neighbors called them. That's who was at the door. It seemed as if they were on his side." Kendra sighed and leaned her head back to the chair. Her voice was monotone, void of any emotion. "After he told them about me being HIV positive and that he felt he had it, they gave him information on where to get tested, and one of them even told him to press charges."

"What? What did he say?"

"We have a court date at the end of February."

Gracie felt sympathy beyond words. She wished she could be there for Kendra more on a deeper level, but her pain wouldn't let her. Gracie asked Kendra if she wanted to reschedule but Kendra insisted they go forward with their meeting.

"Well, these are the figures I've come up with." Gracie stretched the paper across the table to Kendra, who barely glanced at them.

"That's fine." Kendra didn't put up a fight, and they came to a conclusion about the gym and their co-ownership. She already knew things wouldn't work out as they used to. A lot had changed. That was why she had suggested that Gracie buy her out.

Kendra stood and got ready to leave. Gracie walked around the table to a disheveled Kendra.

"Kendra . . . I'm sorry. I'm sorry that I wasn't a friend to you. I had no idea the things that you had gone through. You never told me that your uncle did those things to you—you never opened up about your mom, I just assumed. There are no excuses, but I should have been a better friend."

With no response, Kendra headed at the door.

"Kendra, take care."

"Yeah. You do the same, Gracie."

They embraced in a painful hug. Gracie released Kendra, moved to the side, and let her walk through the door.

After Kendra left the office, Gracie decided to take a few laps around the gym's inside track. After the workout, Gracie went back into her, now very spacious office, to take a quick shower. The office phone rang right before she walked out the door. Just before the last ring, Gracie picked up the receiver, and the other end let out a loud breath and hung up. She assumed that the call must have been misdirected. Gracie hung up and went to the shower.

After she left the gym, Gracie went to the U.S. Post Office and the grocery store to pick out dinner for the night. She received three additional calls on her cell phone with nothing on the other end besides breathing. Figuring that the calls would subside, Gracie didn't mention them to Marcus when he called and confirmed dinner.

"What's cooking, good looking?"

"Aww, aren't you sweet. Flatter me even when you can't see me." Gracie smiled.

Marcus dove in for a fun game. "Now you know I have my spies watching you at all times, Gracie. I can't chance you getting away from me."

"Oh really?"

"Yes, really! They called me on my way back and let me know that you did something different to your hair. They sent me a picture and I likes . . . I likes!"

Gracie was stunned that he knew that she had taken down her braids and returned her relaxed hair to its now lengthy bob. She was lost for words.

"Girl! Look to your right." He drove his truck next to Gracie's car. Marcus couldn't stop laughing as he saw the look on Gracie's face. "I'm sorry, honey. I couldn't help it!"

"Marcus! Ugh." Gracie hung up on her beau and pulled off of the busy highway extension into a gas station's parking lot. The couple got out of their vehicles and embraced.

"I miss you," Marcus sincerely told his girlfriend.

"I miss you more," she kissed back. "I have dinner all picked out. You want to follow me home? I take it that's where you were heading anyhow."

"You're so right. Hey, how did the meeting go?" Marcus asked as he unzipped his nylon jogging suit. He placed the jacket through his window and onto the passenger's seat. Then he got the gas station's window-washing bucket and started on Gracie's car windows.

"It went," Gracie answered as she sat back in her driver's seat. "I'll tell you all about it over dinner."

"I guess it did go alright, since the men in blue didn't contact me," he said, cracking a joke.

"Get out of my way before the men in blue come get me for running over you. See you at the house."

"Right behind you," he said as he returned the brush to its home.

CHAPTER THIRTY-ONE

Gracie was working solely on the business side of Full of Grace. She had finally begun to have a personal life. She spent time reading, exercising, and trying new homemade dishes out on Marcus—even some Marcus wouldn't dare touch. She made time to attend a few of Marcus's football games. When he officially introduced her as his girlfriend, her comfort zone kicked up to a whole new level.

Their bond had grown significantly as they spent more time together. Wednesday night Bible study had become a ritual for them, as well as attending their church homes on alternating Sundays.

One particular Wednesday night, Marcus stunned Gracie when he drove to a restaurant instead of church. Her eyes showed excitement and surprise.

"Marcus, what are we doing here?"

"What do you mean?" Marcus turned to her. "Did y forget that it's Valentine's Day? Besides, we hav had dinner."

Gracie smiled from ear to ear. "What about ch

"Oh, we won't get in trouble for missing one Wednesday night study. What'll you say?'

"Well. Since you talked me into it," Gracie laughed. "Okay."

A valet opened Gracie's door and extended his hand to her. She took it and exited the truck.

Gracie smiled throughout dinner. The restaurant's relaxed atmosphere and happy patrons added to her happiness. She and Marcus sat in an intimate corner, candles illuminating their faces. She didn't think she could be any happier. When Marcus reached inside of his shirt pocket, her eyes widened with curiosity.

"Gracie," Marcus began, "this is not to hold onto you. I'm for that. It's not to keep you. God's for that. But this is to show you that I would love to have you in my life forever.

"This ring is not an engagement ring; it's a promise ring. I promise to be the best boyfriend and friend, period! If you'll allow me, I'd like to stay around as long as I can."

With the softness in her eyes and hope in her heart, Gracie nodded yes. Marcus came around to her and placed the ring on her finger, before hugging her and kissing her forehead.

After dessert, Gracie and Marcus headed out of the restaurant toward the valet. As they stood waiting for Marcus's truck, Gracie spotted a long-time client coming out of the restaurant. She hadn't seen her around the gym, so she decided to say hello.

"Dominique!" Gracie yelled as she waved her arms. "Hey there."

Gracie's smile fell slightly as she walked toward Dominique and noticed her standoffish stance. The petite, older woman stood ramrod straight and her eyes wandered around, never resting on Gracie for too long.

"Uh, hello there," the woman said. She stepped back when Gracie offered her a hug.

A cold chill crept up Gracie's back. For a split second, she shared a confused look with Marcus.

"Oh, okay," Gracie said. "Um, anyway, I've been trying to contact you because I noticed that your membership went inactive. Are you pulling your membership from the gym?"

"Yes. I'm sorry, but yes I am."

Gracie took a tentative step toward Dominique and stopped when the woman's eyes rose.

"May I ask why?" she asked. "Is there something I can help you with? You're a great client and I would hate to see you go."

Dominique attempted to speak, but no words came out. Her husband pulled up and blew the horn. She turned halfway toward the car and stopped.

"The thing is, Gracie," she said, turning to face Gracie and Marcus, "with so many diseases going on in the world, I can't be ignorant and risk my life just for a flatter tummy. I'd rather have a tummy tuck than die in your gym."

Gracie stood in complete astonishment as Dominique rushed into the awaiting car. Not even Marcus's reassuring hug and warmth could remove her stunned reaction.

Marcus practically had to carry Gracie from the car to her apartment. Inside, Marcus sat her down and made a pot of coffee.

"Was the lady talking about Kendra?" Marcus asked, once he brought in two mugs of coffee, sugar, and cream.

"I think that's exactly what she was talking about," Gracie answered. She sipped her coffee. "I just don't know how she got her information."

"You don't think Kendra told, do you?"

"I doubt it. She's so jittery about anyone knowing about her, she wouldn't risk it. Dillian's out of the question, too. He wouldn't do anything to hurt me intentionally. Maybe it's whoever keeps calling and hanging up?" Gracie was now getting the calls every day. Marcus looked at Gracie in surprise since he knew nothing about the calls. The phone rang.

"Speaking of which," Gracie said, "can you get that while I use the little girl's room?"

"Sure," Marcus said, making a mental note to ask Gracie about the hang-up calls.

When Marcus answered the phone, a gruff voice yelled, "Can you be so nice to tell your little girlfriend that her whole world will crumble down once her ex-man and friend are revealed to the public? Dominique Watson is just one of many who will walk away from her business."

"Who is this?" Marcus asked. He stared at the phone as the voice was replaced by a dial tone.

Gracie reentered the room and found Marcus still staring at the phone.

"Who was it, Marcus?"

"I don't know." He hung up the phone. "Whoever it was made it clear that they were going public about Dillian and Kendra."

Gracie fell onto the couch. "What?" she asked with her voice in its highest pitch. "What is going on?" She straightened herself on the sofa and looked at Marcus. "I've actually been getting these hang-up calls, but I didn't know it was going to get this deep."

"You should have told me Gracie. This person is trying to ruin you." Marcus shook his head and sighed. "I hate to say this, Gracie, but I think it's Michelle that's been calling you."

"Do you really think she's that hard up? I just can't believe that she would go through all this."

"Gracie, the girl had papers already drawn up for me, ready for me to sue you." Taking a breath, Marcus continued, "A while back, Michelle invited herself over to the house and pulled out some paperwork, what I thought was bogus paperwork. She had Dillian's test results . . . she had some paperwork, a contract I think, that she wanted me to sign in order to sue you."

"What! She went that far?"

"Yeah. I'm afraid so."

Gracie didn't know where she was going to get the guts to do so, but she needed to warn both Dillian and Kendra. Fasting and praying were her only options to find peace to help them. Even though they had given her nothing but pain, Gracie knew what Jesus would do.

On a daily basis, Gracie sought after God's heart. She needed to hear from Him and to go in the way He wanted her to go. It was a fight she had to fight and wouldn't let go until she heard from the One who had pulled her through in so many ways. Without a doubt, Gracie knew God's voice.

CHAPTER THIRTY-TWO

Gracie called ahead to Dillian to let him know she was coming over to talk, she told him about Marcus, how he had returned in her life to support her. She asked Dillian if it would be okay if he came along with her.

"No problem, Gracie. That'll be fine."

Gracie and Marcus made quick tracks. They arrived at Dillian's new apartment in record time. Boxes and furniture crowded the place, and there was only enough room for the trio to stand and walk around.

"Hey, guys," Dillian said when he opened the door. "Come on in."

Marcus extended his hand to Dillian and said, "How's it going, man?"

Dillian offered Marcus a slight smile and shook his hand. "I'm doing," he replied. "Thanks for asking."

As soon as the door to the apartment closed, Gracie walked in a few steps and turned to face Dillian.

"Look, Gracie. I haven't seen or heard from you . . . since. Umm. I'm sorry—." Taking a look over at Marcus, Dillian knew that he couldn't allow himself to become embarrassed. "I've been praying and I just want you to know that I'm asking God to settle your heart. I could possibly care less about my end . . . I just want you to be at peace." He sensed Gracie's uneasiness. "Well, I just needed to get that off of my chest. You sounded urgent over the phone. What can I help you with?"

"Well, it's nothing for you to help me out with, but maybe you can help yourself," she said, not even touching on his comment. "I've been getting calls warning me that someone is going to go public about your situation."

"What?" Dillian's eyes bulged. "Who did you tell?"

Gracie threw a hand up to her chest and looked offended. "Dillian, I didn't tell anyone!" she said. "Don't even go there. Whoever it is plans to go public about you and Kendra, but it's all to get back at me—to hurt me and my business."

Dillian sat on a box and grabbed his head with both hands. "What in the world am I supposed to do?" he whispered.

Marcus stepped in between Gracie and Dillian and sat down on a nearby vacant chair.

"How about going public yourself, before this person does?" he asked.

"Are you crazy? Excuse me, man, but I've lost customers just from missing in action. Imagine when they hear that I am HIV positive."

"You can't get it from working out," Marcus said.

"I know that, you know that, but people are not trying to hear any of that."

"Dillian," Gracie cut in. "It really doesn't seem like you have much of a choice at this point. You either do it, or someone will do it for you."

Dillian closed his eyes and thought about it. He knew it would be devastating to his clients if they found out from the media instead of him. People would leave either way, but he knew that more would desert him if he wasn't up front about his sickness.

"I guess you're right," he said after a while. "But what if I lose everything?"

Gracie opened her mouth to speak, but Marcus answered. "Then we'll be right there to help you pick up the pieces." Gracie turned to Marcus and gave him a smile that showed her love.

Dillian shook his head in disbelief at Marcus and Gracie's sincerity.

"You two don't have to do this," Dillian said, "but I'm glad you are."

After chatting for a few minutes, Gracie and Marcus got ready to leave. Marcus opened the door and headed to the car before Gracie.

"Hey, Gracie. I really am glad you came. I've been thinking about you," Dillian said. "I really am sorry about all of this and I pray that you will forgive me one day."

"Dillian. I've already forgiven you. It's time for you to start forgiving yourself." Gracie placed a friendly kiss on Dillian's cheek and shared a long, friendly hug with her ex before she left out of the door.

The meeting with Kendra didn't go as well. As soon as Gracie told Kendra the news, Kendra flipped and refused to see Gracie's logic.

"No, uh uh," she argued. "If they want to tell my business, let them go ahead. I'll deny it! Gracie, I haven't even told my family. Heck, I've barely let it sink in myself. No!"

"What do you think is going to happen when you go

to court?" Gracie asked. "There will be legal documents. Anyone will be able to get a hold of them."

"If they do, they do." Kendra flopped down on her sofa, refusing to look at Gracie or Marcus. "I can't do it. I won't!"

Gracie sat in a chair opposite Kendra. Marcus's hand rested on Gracie's shoulder.

"I'm really afraid, Gracie," Kendra whispered as she scooted to the front of the sofa. "I know all of my information will be out there once I go to court. What if they find me guilty?"

Gracie took Kendra's hands and squeezed them. "With the expertise your lawyers have, it doesn't sound likely to me."

"And any additional help you need," Marcus added, "I will be there for you, along with Gracie."

Gracie's heart swelled at Marcus's love for people who had caused her so much pain. Gracie and Kendra hugged, and Gracie was filled with a renewed hope. Gracie knew that her peace with Dillian and Kendra could only come from above. She invoked God in a silent prayer.

CHAPTER THIRTY-THREE

When Marcus and Gracie pulled up to her apartment, they sat in the car for just a moment while Marcus told how proud he was of her.

"You did it, huh?"

"Yep . . . I did it. I still can't believe it though."

Marcus walked around his car and opened the door for Gracie. They proceeded inside.

"Honey, I know it's not going to be an easy task," Marcus said, "but remember, *He* never said it would be."

"I know." Gracie sighed. "I just can't believe that I am even considering helping them out. They both cheated on me."

Gracie leaned into Marcus and allowed him to cradle her in his arms.

"I know it hurts, Gracie," Marcus whispered, "but if this didn't happen, I wouldn't be holding you right now. I know it sounds redundant and an easy answer, but I was made to love you and to help you through the rough times. Just lean on me, okay?"

"I want to, Marcus, I really do, and I am, but I have to let you know that I am afraid. I can't keep putting my all into people and then they let me down. I thought life got easier as you got older."

"*He* never said that either. And how about you not put your trust in me, or anyone else? Just put your trust in the Lord. Pray about everything, not something, but everything. He'll let you know what you need to do. Until you tell me differently, I'll be here for you."

"I know you will."

Eventually, Gracie allowed herself to relax in Marcus's arms. As she drifted, she really felt in her heart and soul that Marcus was meant for her.

Gracie was glad that she was with Marcus and that he had come into her life when he had. With Marcus, life was different. She could tell he was genuine. Everything came with ease. She had received the answer from above: he was the one. They were equally yoked.

All in all, she planned on moving at a pace that she didn't design herself. She wanted the full effect of what God had for her and wanted to be cleansed of her past. Reading God's Word allowed her to know that He had forgiven her for all of her past wrongs and would guide her to be who He wanted her to be. Committing herself to God and living a holy and healthy life was what filled her agenda.

CHAPTER THIRTY-FOUR

Gracie called the local news station. She spoke with one of the managers about the news conference she wanted to set up for Dillian.

"Oh, Ms. Gregory, I'm sorry, but the timeslot has been filled. Why don't you come by the station at three o'clock instead?"

"But I was previously told to come at two o'clock. Why was I moved?"

"I must apologize, Ms. Gregory. I don't have the answer for you on that matter. On the schedule it had down that a Michelle Eisenhower is to come in with her proposal for a press conference as well."

Gracie knew what Michelle was up to. "Oh really? Okay. Three o'clock will work out fine."

Gracie hung up the phone and briefly considered calling Marcus and getting his opinion on whether she should confront Michelle. She knew he would tell her not to worry about Michelle, but Gracie had no choice. Her friends and her livelihood were involved.

As Gracie sat at her desk and doodled, she knew she

had to pull out all her connections to right Michelle's wrongs. For the most part, she liked to play fair, but she knew that desperate times called for desperate measures. She picked up the phone and began to dial.

Gracie arrived at her appointment with the news station a bit early. She leaned against her car and waited for Michelle to leave the news station.

Taking her tight strides to her luxury car, Michelle had no idea that Gracie was waiting. She gave her outfit a look over to make sure she had indeed been presentable at her appointment. She had on the right attire to get next to the manager on shift, making sure she got exactly what she needed.

As she got closer to her car, Michelle became aware of Gracie. "Oh. Hi there, Gracie," Michelle said slowing her stride. "Is there something I can help you with?"

"Hmm," Gracie replied, "no, not really. I just thought I'd wait out here for you. I figured there was no need for a big scene inside."

"Umm, a big scene?" Michelle threw her 'you stole my man' attitude at Gracie and she played nonchalant. "What are you talking about? A big scene?"

Gracie kept her cool, but the hotness showed on her face. Gracie let Michelle have it.

"I know it's you, Michelle! Just like you blocked my two o'clock appointment, I know it's you that's representing Sean. You're not the only one with connections."

Michelle made it to her car in record time. Not responding until she got close enough, Michelle unlocked her car door.

"Gracie," she began, "I have plenty of clients, and yes, some may even be named Sean, but as far as you saying 'you know it's me,' I have no idea what you're talking about," she concluded with a sly smirk pasted on her face.

"Sure you don't. You mean you're not the one calling my home or having someone else do it?"

"No," Michelle said as she placed her purse and briefcase in the backseat of her car. She turned and threw her hands up onto her hips. "No, it's not. Why would I call your home?"

"Because you think that I stole Marcus from you. That would be one good reason, wouldn't it? That's why."

"Don't be so silly, Gracie," Michelle stated as she opened her car door. "It's not that serious. Besides, Marcus isn't all that. He likes plain things in life . . . if you know what I mean."

"Sure, I know what you mean, and I'll let that go over my head. But if it's not that serious, then why are you trying to ruin my business and ruin other people's lives?"

"Ruin your business? Other people's lives? I could care less. If your clients are leaving, it's not because of me, Gracie!" Michelle found the courage to defend herself.

Gracie let Michelle know that she was busted. "How'd you know they were leaving, Michelle? You're sick and the game is over!"

Michelle felt cornered. She took steps backward and got into her car.

". . . And that's not what Dominique says." Gracie walked up to the car and leaned down to the window, looking Michelle eye to eye. "For Valentine's Day, Marcus took me to dinner, and I happened to run into Dominique there. I asked her about her pulling her membership. In so many words, she told me why. Long story short, I called a couple of days ago and she explained that you called her out of nowhere, and let her know what was going on. So, Michelle, what is going on?"

Michelle sat and gripped her steering wheel harder than she knew. She tried to hide her fear but failed.

"I don't know what you're talking about. You wanted Marcus, you got him! And as far as he's concerned, I was just trying to be a friend to him, letting him know about your status. It didn't seem like you ever would. The same with Dominique. People need to know!"

"My status? For your information, I don't have a status, and if I did, that would be my decision to tell people, not yours. If you're that hard up for a man, I really feel sorry for you. But just like I took up for myself with Dominique and got her back as a client, I'm going to take up for my friends. So you can try what you want, it doesn't matter. You won't prosper from it!"

"Yeah right! Just watch me!" Michelle yelled out as she gunned her car. Gracie jumped back just in time to avoid being a hit-and-run casualty.

CHAPTER THIRTY-FIVE

The Tuesday before Kendra's court appearance, Gracie spent time with Kendra, Dillian, and Marcus. The four had brunch and discussed Dillion's upcoming, news conference.

"Sean and Michelle? How'd that happen?" Kendra questioned.

When Gracie told Dillian and Kendra about Michelle representing Sean, Kendra couldn't believe it.

Gracie shrugged her shoulders. "Who knows? Michelle is capable of a lot, I've learned. Marcus and I pretty much figured it was Michelle to begin with. She gave him the information so that he would start questioning me himself."

"I knew something was fishy with that little Miss Prissy," Kendra said with her nose in the air.

"Yep," Gracie agreed. "You were right."

"Don't worry about it, Kendra," Marcus said as he patted her hand. "No matter what happens in the courtroom, we'll all be in there to back you up."

"Yes, we surely will," Dillian chimed in. "I'm ready.

Last week, I sent memos to my clients letting them know about my status. All but two remained under my training. One of my clients even came forward and told me that he was HIV positive as well. His story gives me hope."

"Well, I don't know how much hope I have," Kendra said, "but I am very thankful that you can be as strong as you are." Kendra looked directly at Gracie and gave her a small smile. "I've always known you were strong. You're the best. Though I have failed you as a friend, your forgiveness and support shows the kind of person I've always known you were. Most people wouldn't, well, couldn't do it. I thank you, Gracie."

"Gracie, I thank you too," Dillian said. "I let you down and I'm paying the ultimate price for it. I'm still wrestling with what I have done, of course. Lord knows if it weren't for your initial concern, I don't know if I would be here at this moment. But mostly, if you hadn't forgiven me, I know I wouldn't have found strength so early in my battle."

Dillian patted Marcus on the back and added, "Marcus, you're a lucky man. You two belong together."

Marcus reached for Gracie's hand and smiled.

"It's all about Gracie," he said. "I just want to see her happy. She's worth a million, you know? She's a good woman, and I've always known that."

"Oh you have?" Gracie asked through tears.

"Yes. I have."

"Well. Thank you, Kendra. Dillian, just so that you know, it's a journey. You guys have hurt me deeply. Real deep. My life has changed dramatically because of you. Thankfully, God has and is helping me through this trial.

"Praying to God helped me forgive you two. And honestly, I knew that one day I would forgive you, but

I thought it would be years from now. Then He spoke to me and told me now was the time to forgive. Not because you two are sick, but because I know not the day of my own departure. I had to forgive for my own sake." Dabbing her eyes, Gracie continued.

"Honestly, after this ordeal, I don't know what can become of this, but just to let you know, I'm letting the Lord lead me. That doesn't mean I won't have love for the two of you, but I do believe this was a season I had to go through. If God says otherwise, you'll be the first two to know."

They all joined in a group, roundtable hug.

CHAPTER THIRTY-SIX

Shortly after the verdict was revealed in Kendra's case, the news conference that was scheduled to follow was cancelled. The judge placed a gag order on the proceedings, prohibiting Michelle and Sean from speaking of the incident outside of the courtroom doors.

Kendra had been prepared to defend her HIV status to the public. But with the gag order, she didn't have to. Instead, they went to plan 'B,' in which Gracie stepped up to the plate.

Gracie wanted to go ahead and discuss her experience abroad, hoping to help someone else along the way. In place of the press conference, Gracie set up a speaking engagement at the fitness center.

The set up was not formal. Gracie nervously went straight to the podium and began speaking to the medium-sized crowd.

"Good afternoon, I'm Gracie Gregory and I would like to thank you all for coming out. On behalf of two very close friends, I have invited a courageous woman to speak to all of us today about her life. Her story is dear to me.

"This whole *incident* started months ago with what I thought was a problem that only affected myself. It quickly grew to affect two other people who are very close to me. Although HIV is a well-known disease, at that time, it hadn't been in my life. Because of life's *unique* circumstances, I had to endure the scare, wondering if I had the disease. I, like many, had to wait for my fate to be revealed. During my time of personal circumstances, I'm sure you'll have heard the rumors, people telling you about me, before I knew about me . . . Well, because of the support of my family and the other parties involved, I was able to stand through all the trials. Not only stand, but rebuild what I thought was broken. Many of my clients who left, I'd like to say, thank you for coming back. I want to say thank you, not because you came because of my negative HIV test results, but because you are loyal. It's the genuiness from loyal people that makes the world go around.

"Before I bring this great speaker on stage, I'd like to take time out to give a public appreciation to my parents and to my boyfriend, Marcus. It was definitely their strength, sweat, and tears that pulled me through."

Gracie smiled and a let a few tears escape as the crowd exploded in applause.

"Without further ado," Gracie continued, "I'd like to present someone who counseled with me through email because she herself couldn't get to me quick enough. Someone who knows the everyday walk with both HIV and AIDS and is not afraid to talk about her journey. Someone who is dedicated to living. Please give a warm welcome to my new confidante and friend, Lydia Sketchel."

Lydia stood from the fourth row and walked to the

stage. "Ooohs" and "aaahs" emitted from the audience. It was hard for them to imagine that this woman, looking every bit like Miss America, was suffering from HIV and AIDS. Before Gracie passed the podium to Lydia, she offered her new friend a warm, tight hug.

When Gracie had contacted Lydia via her website, they started an on-line relationship. Eventually Gracie was putting together a seminar that would showcase Lydia's and her own story about HIV.

"Thank you, thank you," Lydia said. She leaned closer to the microphone and added, "To the whisperers, I even thank you!"

Nervous laughter filtered through the audience.

"I'm Lydia Sketchel and yes, I have full-blown AIDS. I just call it AIDS. There's no half-blown AIDS or no in-between as I last checked, just AIDS.

"To tell you a little about myself first, I'm thirty-two, a full-time lecturer, and a survivor for eight years. I was twenty-four years old when I found out that I was a carrier. I found out about my status from my very first pap smear. When I was told to come by the office for more tests and that I had an option to bring someone along, I didn't think anything of it. I simply went.

"When I heard that I was HIV positive, I did what just about anyone would. I lost my mind. I denied my results and I lost my mind again. When asked if I could write down possible transmitters or if I knew who had infected me, I wrote my name over and over on the dotted line because I, in fact, had slept with men without protection. I was now a transmitter. Of all eight men I had slept with from twenty-one to twenty-three, the first had infected me, and I, in turn, had infected the other seven. I had passed along a disease I didn't know I was carrying, all because sex felt better without a condom.

"I hadn't infected my boyfriend at the time because he had insisted that we make love with protection only or not at all.

"When it came time for me to sit down and figure out who could have been my transmitter, it was a hard task. I could have contracted the disease from anywhere. From casual dating, spring break trips, one night stands. I didn't know where to start. Thinking of all the names and the "loves of my life," my brain scrambled even more. I started with my boyfriend from my junior year in college who was madly in love with me, but just *had* to transfer to another university on the other side of the world. He wasn't easy to locate.

"By the time all of my research was complete and all of my anonymous letters were mailed out, I found my ex-boyfriend. He was dead and had been for six months . . . ever since he'd left me. He killed himself because he was not able to live with his status.

"After my anonymous letters were received, my phone began to ring. I don't know what made these guys automatically think that I had sent the letters. Maybe it was my freakiness, my happy-go-lucky way of life, or my carefree attitude about sex. Whatever it was, they contacted me. Not all of them, but the ones who did threatened me so badly that I eventually had to get the law involved.

"On my thirtieth birthday I received a present that couldn't be returned no matter how many receipts came with it. My HIV grew to AIDS, which meant that the expensive drugs I was prescribed to take for HIV doubled, and I would be taking them for the rest of my life. That was two years ago. Just when I had adjusted to the HIV medication, I had a start all over with the side effects of nausea, diarrhea, fatigue, and severe dry skin. My body started to do its own thing, things I would have never guessed it could do. I won't bore you with those details. Look it up. It's in the book.

"After suffering through different medications that did no good to my body, my doctors finally found the correct brands and dosages for me. So far, they soothe me. Not to get too technical, but I have had problems with pneumonia, my immune count dropping, and AIDS-related lymphoma, a disease in which cancer cells are found in my system. Lucky for me, the tumors found on my body have been benign. I believe it's because I have a will to live in spite of my situation.

"Just like I have a will to live, I'm sure you in the audience do as well. But it would be easier for you if you would start now. Don't wait until you have positive test results before you decide to live. If you're sitting there and you feel that you are not a tramp or wild child as I have made myself out to be, think again. From high school to college, the average relationship may last six months. Every six months for four years is enough time to come across the wrong person. Not to mention the people in between.

"If you say you know your partner, just how well do you know him or her? What if your partner is a reformed heroin addict? And believe me, addicts come in all shapes and sizes. Today, heterosexual groups are growing in the HIV positive category because people are playing games and having unprotected sex. Husbands are having girlfriends on the side; wives are having boyfriends on the side.

"Even though the homosexual community has always been blamed for the start of all this madness, it's also the individuals that hide their *real sexuality* from their loved ones who continue to help spread this deadly disease. It's time to be true and safe. For women, the statistics show that in the last ten years, the reported number of cases has tripled. HIV infection is now one of the leading causes of death among African-American women from their mid-twenties to their mid-forties, but please don't think that any other age is immune. We all need to be alert and aware.

"As I conclude, when I think about my situation, through my sickness and rough spots, and sometimes those can be plenty, I look back and know that I am blessed, and I am thankful for that. I may have had it worse than some, but not more than others. I can truly say that I'm happy through my weak moments, through my crying times, through my shallow breaths, through my doctor's visits, my drug intake. Mostly through my lectures I am moved with the feeling that someone, even if it is just one person, has taken my life . . . and even my beauty," she added with a giggle, "and turned his or her life around.

"People, don't do it for me, do it for you. Know that a negative status starts with you and the care you have for your life. Protect yourself."

After the applause in the air halted, Kendra and Dillian made their way to the stage. Gracie sat, speechless, as Dillian walked to the podium and took the microphone. Kendra was a few steps behind him.

"Far too long," he began, "I have let Gracie carry the crutch of my problem alone. I knew one day I would come out and tell my story, I just never knew it would be this soon. I am HIV positive." Dillian took a breath and allowed the crowd to settle. As the bulbs from the news cameras flashed, Dillian winced.

He looked at Gracie, his tears matched hers. "Today, I hope that I can help someone save his or her life with my story. As you all know, I am Dillian McNab— Mr. Universe, to many. I have been around the world, competed in too many competitions to count, yet none of my success helped me out with being able to dodge becoming infected with HIV.

"As much as I would like to say I didn't get the disease by doing wrong, I can't. I contracted HIV by using steroids through needles to help me compete in the bodybuilding world. It was my decision to come out of retirement and start competing again. When I did, I trusted someone who I thought was a friend, to supply me with the drugs. At first, I blamed him, but I later realized it was much deeper than that. If you don't remember anything else I say today, please remember that anything you do in the dark is not worth living through in the light. I was the only one to blame. I made the decision to take steroids.

"My relationship with Gracie Gregory was a relationship that had evolved into an engagement that was to become a marriage. Of course, that didn't happen. I thank God that my stupidity didn't mean the end of Gracie's life. I wouldn't be able to live with myself knowing that I gave her a death sentence that she didn't deserve. I call her a hero because that is what she is. Gracie saved her own life. In our relationship, Gracie made it known that she cared about herself. She made sure that she protected herself in every manner that she could. I pouted about it, but Gracie never backed down. She always had her head in the right direction and allowed God to be her guide. Her intelligent decisions saved her life. Let that be a lesson. I will forever be in debt to Gracie."

Kendra walked to Dillian and gave him a hug. His shoulders shook as he sobbed without embarrassment. Kendra took Dillian's hand, and together, they walked to Gracie. Gracie stood after receiving a kiss from Marcus and she, Kendra, and Dillian shared a long, hard hug.

While in the embrace, Kendra whispered to Gracie, "I thank you so much for all you've done for me, Gracie, despite all the wrong I've done to you."

Gracie understood why Kendra couldn't yet reveal her fate to the public. She was thankful that Kendra didn't come out. She knew that if the public knew about Dillian *and* Kendra's illness, they would badger Gracie to death about how she was able to comfort people who had hurt her in such horrific ways.

Gracie knew that not many people would understand why she was able to stand through her storm, and that was perfectly all right with her. She knew that her stance was only possible through her tolerance. God had given her the test He did because He knew she could pass it. Gracie had been the one chosen to stand though what many possibly couldn't. Indeed she had been able to conquer all through one source: by the grace of God.

EPILOGUE

With the first lecture, two years, and six HIV tests behind them, Gracie and Marcus were blessed to consummate their love with marriage. Marcus respected and loved Gracie as he said he would. God's grace was sufficient in their lives.

The months turned into years. Seeing how love had conquered all for Marcus and Gracie, Kendra and Dillian clung to each other and allowed mutual feelings to develop over time. With the past behind her, nothing distracted Gracie from her future. All she knew was that she needed Marcus; and Kendra and Dillian obviously needed each other.

Even when Kendra and Dillian's dating grew into an engagement and then marriage, nothing changed. Granted, the couples only socialized at charity events or lectures promoting HIV/AIDS awareness. But the new marriage didn't bring them closer or push Gracie or Marcus farther away. There were still no hard feelings. If Dillian or Kendra ever needed her, Gracie had enough room in her heart to be there for the two.

Waiting until their wedding night to be sexually intimate, Gracie and Marcus were blessed by God. Before they entered their honeymoon suite, Marcus stopped short to speak words into his new bride's ears that he had practiced over and over in his heart.

"Gracie, I love you. It's a love that is felt from my soul, my being . . . who I am. It's more than just words that are said on an everyday basis. These words are sacred. I promise to love you thoroughly and without recourse. If you're worrying about anything, I want you to let go and let God. Let go of everything that we have gone through individually and everything we've gone through together and give your heart and your mind to God and then me." With a soft kiss on her forehead, Marcus allowed Gracie to speak.

"I love you, Marcus."

Marcus told Gracie that he respected her for looking out for him for the past two years and thanked her for looking out for his future as well. He then let her know that the vows they had taken united them as one.

"When I love you tonight, I love you for all that you are. Just like I said in my vow to you, I meant it, Gracie."

He wanted Gracie to understand that all the protection she had gotten for the both of them for their honeymoon vacation was not needed. After he rocked and swayed her in his arms until she felt the passion in his heart for herself, Gracie prayed and then agreed.

Being beautiful and whole is one thing, but being complete is full circle. Gracie was now beautiful, whole, and complete. The truth came out when she had the privilege in announcing a honeymoon baby three months later. When the baby inside grew to two, she knew for sure that she was blessed.

With a new marriage, a baby on the way, and the grand opening of Full of Grace II Spa and Gym, Gracie knew that her life was right where it needed to be.

Discussion Questions

1. Do you think that Dillian was being fair in his attempt to run from the problem instead of staying and discussing everything with Gracie?

2. Could it have been too difficult or embarrassing for him to share such a secret with his fiancé?

3. Do you believe that Gracie compromised her Christianity in the relationship with Dillian? What about her relationship with Marcus?

4. When she received the phone calls from the health department, do you believe Gracie knew deep down that something was wrong, or if she really believed that OSHA had been calling for the gym?

5. Was it fair for Gracie to mix business with pleasure when she realized that a client was attached to her ex-boyfriend?

6. When Gracie found out about Kendra and her relationship with Sean, was it appropriate for her to confront her friend about their business? Was Kendra wrong to keep her lifestyle from her friend?

7. Do you feel that Marcus was meant to be in Gracie's life and that destiny brought him back around just when she needed him most? Could she have handled the situation without him?

8. Was Michelle wrong for prying into the lives of

Gracie and Dillian just so her chances of being with Marcus wouldn't be tainted?

9. How do you think Gracie would have reacted if the counselor had given her different results?

10. The way Sean reacted to Kendra, was it a realistic action? How else could he have dealt with the situation?

Urban Christian His Glory Book Club!

Established January 2007, **UC His Glory Book Club** is another way by which to introduce to the literary world, Urban Book's much-anticipated new imprint, **Urban Christian** and its authors. We are an online book club supporting Urban Christian authors by purchasing, reading and providing written reviews of the authors' books that are read. *UC His Glory* welcomes both men and women of the literary world who have a passion for reading Christian based fiction.

UC His Glory is the brainchild of Joylynn Jossel, author and Executive Editor of Urban Christian and Kendra Norman-Bellamy, author and Director of Talent & Operations for Urban Christian. The book club will provide support, positive feedback, encouragement and a forum whereby members can openly discuss and review the literary works of Urban Christian authors. In the future, we anticipate broadening our spectrum of services to include: online author chats, author spotlights, interviews with your favorite Urban Christian author(s), special online groups for *UC Book Club* members, ability to post reviews on the website and amazon.com, membership ID cards, *UC His Glory* Yahoo Group and much more.

Even though there will be no membership fees attached to becoming a member of *UC His Glory Book Club*, we do expect our members to be active, committed and to follow the guidelines of the Book Club.

UC His Glory members pledge to:

- Follow the guidelines of *UC His Glory Book Club*.
- Provide input, opinions, and reviews that build up, rather than tear down.
- Commit to purchasing, reading and discussing featured book(s) of the month.
- Agree not to miss more than three consecutive online monthly meetings.
- Respect the Christian beliefs of *UC His Glory Book Club*.
- Believe that Jesus is the Christ, Son of the Living God

We look forward to the online fellowship.

Many Blessings to You!

Shelia E. Lipsey
President
UC His Glory Book Club

**Visit the official Urban Christian Book Club website at
www.uchisglorybookclub.net